SURRENDER

Stephen   Burke

DAYBUE PUBLISHING INK
SAN FRANCISCO   SUN VALLEY

DayBue Publishing Ink

2107 Van Ness Avenue
Suite 104
San Francisco, CA 94109

First DayBue Publishing Ink Edition 1999

DayBue Publishing Ink, design, and logo are trademarks
of DayBue Publishing Ink.

Cover design by Elizabeth Day
Cover illustration by Carly Hirsch

Printed in Canada

Library of Congress Catalog No. 98-93802

ISBN 0-9668940-0-6

For Bill Ryan, who treated me as an adult
when I saw myself as a child;
and
For Marie, who treated me as a child
when I saw myself as an adult

Acknowledgements

I thank ... the wonderfully dedicated and passionate people at DayBue Publishing for their vision, commitment, and talents ... the amazing editorial team of EB and Chris for raising the literary quality of this work ... Christina for her love and insights ... Thomas for his example and his editorial assistance (better late than never) ... Elizabeth, Kara and Mother for risking what they had earned in order to move me ... my winged friend for never leaving me alone ... Marie, Peter, Mark and Cédric for choosing me. And, most of all, I thank Armelle for journeying with me—sometimes at my side, sometimes on my back and sometimes carrying me. Armelle proves true the aphorism that the journey is more important than the destination.

Surrender

Me voilà. Here I am, Eric Pétris, telling the story of my life, or rather, the story of my death. I am still not quite sure. It all began October 28, 1992, in a clinic in Lyon, France—the day after my wife, Camille, went into labor, the day our first child was born. It may seem strange that my story would begin with the birth of my daughter. I'd often heard that having children changes your life. That's like saying that taking a nap on the TGV tracks changes your bone structure.

There was no warning in the early morning hours of that day that anything unusual—much less, extraordinary—was at hand. The hospital in Lyon was receiving its nightly stipend of drunk drivers and their victims. There was a child who had awakened in the middle of the night crying of abdominal pains, now sleeping peacefully as his parents awaited the results of his blood test. An elderly man, suffering from chest pains, was casually wheeled into the x-ray room. All very routine. All very quiet.

Except for what was about to occur in Room 203.

I was sacrificing my hand so that Camille could unload some of her pain on me. I was awed by her courage, especially by her stamina. She was in her sixteenth hour of labor. The waves of contractions were pounding her body, their rapid cadence offering her little time to catch a breath. It couldn't possibly be much longer, I thought. *Please, dear God, do something to end this.* I wanted the marathon to end as much for my wife as for me. I was going on twenty-six hours without sleep. I didn't know how much longer I could keep my eyes open.

I looked down at my hands. Camille's elegant, thin fingers gripped me more tightly than any brute's handshake. I had lost all feeling in my fingers an hour earlier.

Every time I drifted to sleep, she would yank me back to consciousness.

The latest contraction of her abdomen tapered off and her bloodshot eyes opened. She turned to me. "I can't do this anymore."

"Soon, *chérie*. You're almost there." I wondered where the hell the nurse had gone.

"*Non!*" Her head shook emphatically. "I can't go on."

I swallowed. I was responsible for her pain. The realization sucked the breath from me. My ego had swelled with that illogical machismo that every man experiences upon first impregnating his wife—*my boys can swim*. As foreign as such a thought is to a woman, it's no more bizarre than the mentality that has fueled wars throughout the ages. Same thought process, different scale. At that moment, however, my pride at having fathered a child, at being a fertile, virile man was nowhere to be found. *Look what I've done!* was all I could think. Like my father and his father before him, I took pride in my role as provider and protector. And, yet, I was of no help to my wife when she was in more pain than I had ever thought possible to survive. To know that this pain was my doing only made me feel smaller—less of a man. It was a silly thought, but at least I was *feeling* something.

"You can do it. I'll help you."

Her wide, accusing eyes told me what I realized as soon as the words escaped my lips. Nice thought, terrible timing. I shrunk a little more.

"How are you going to help me? *Eh*, Eric?"

The monitor caught my eye. The numbers on the screen were rising and, as if on cue, Camille grimaced and snapped shut the vice over my hand. "Can you feel this?" she yelled. Her eyes remained open this time, staring maliciously at me. "How are you going to help me? Are you going to deliver this baby?"

I realized that my stupidity had actually served her—albeit unintentionally. She was angry and, momentarily at least, less aware of the pain. But just as suddenly, she turned away and sat up with a start. "*Oh, mon dieu!*"

"What?"

"I want to push."

"*Non!*" I screamed. "Wait." I ran to the door.

"Don't leave me."

"Doctor! Nurse!" I yelled down the hallway. "Somebody, hurry! My wife wants to push!"

Within thirty seconds the medical team was into their well rehearsed maneuvers. Like a championship rugby team, each person knew where the other was and anticipated what moves the others would make. I held my wife's hand and watched. What had resembled a modestly comfortable hotel room was instantly transformed into an operating room. A large spot light was lowered from its recessed hiding place. A cart was wheeled out of a closet with what looked like sadistic metal instruments of torture. Suddenly, the obstetrician pushed a button and the bed holding my wife began to rise. In order to maintain my hold of her hand, I had to stand. Then, a third of the bed fell away and stirrups were installed. Camille seemed oblivious. But I, unfortunately, saw every detail. The blood drained from my head as I watched. I felt weak and light-headed. The intensity of the moment was beginning to overwhelm me. I could feel my body shutting down.

"Sit down, Monsieur Pétris," the doctor ordered, noting my pallor. "I can't take care of both of you at once."

Camille was in tears. Her back arched in pain.

I was minutes away from meeting my first child. It was one of life's defining moments—the sort that cannot be imagined in advance but the effects of which echo forever after. I could not stay on my feet. I so desperately wanted to be part of it. I wanted to help—well, maybe not help, but at least witness the moment. I wanted to be strong. But the power of what was happening hit me as hard and as unexpectedly as a white squall coming in off the Atlantic.

My legs gave out and I dropped to the chair. My head fell against the side of the bed. I tried to maintain my grasp of Camille's hand, but the angle was awkward and she pulled away. I felt at once inebriated and omniscient. I knew it was not the medieval instruments the doctors were brandishing, nor the prospect of blood and afterbirth that robbed me of my strength. A squeamish man, I was not. It was something more ... more supernatural that was happening. I felt as though I was in the presence of greatness. Perhaps, this is how it feels to come face-to-face with God, I thought. I rolled my head to the side. Why were the doctor and nurses so nonchalant? Didn't they sense it? I wondered if my wife felt what I did. Of course not. She was in agony. She didn't have the luxury of losing her mind.

"*Je t'aime*," I whispered to her, knowing that Camille couldn't hear me. "I'm sorry I can't do it for you. I'm sorry I'm no help now, but ... I love you. I love you. I love you." Tears came to my eyes with each repetition of the phrase. I realized for the first time what the words meant. I actually *felt* what it was to love. "*Je t'aime. Je t'aime.*" The power of the moment gave way to the power of agape that was coursing through my body. I began to rise from the chair. "*Je t'aime*," I continued to call out until I was once again standing over my wife.

Camille ignored me. Her face was crimson from the strain of pushing. I smiled at her. I caressed her forehead, wiping away the sweat. "*Je t'aime.*" She was breathing quickly now. Just a quick break before the final leg. "*Je t'aime*."

She looked up at me, her eyes pained, but strong. No sound came from her lips, but she mouthed her response, "I love you, too." Her eyes were unlike anything I'd ever seen. They took on a life of their own. They seemed to penetrate me, siphoning from me the extra fuel she needed to make it a few meters more.

"*Je t'aime*," I repeated.

She nodded. No, I realized, she wasn't nodding. She was rocking on the bed, summoning willpower and strength. Her eyes holding me, she bore down. She clenched her teeth for several seconds, and then, shook the walls of the clinic with a primeval wail.

Instantly, I sensed something behind me. I turned quickly. My eyes fell upon our daughter. She was purple and wet, a mop of slick black hair on her head. Her precious mouth opened wide and her chin quivered with a cry in response to her mother's. But I heard no sounds. I did not even notice the blood and other fluids adorning my little girl. All I saw was a vibrating bright light in the shape of an infant.

"Monsieur Pétris?" the doctor called out. "Monsieur Pétris?"

My head jerked up from the bed as if I'd never left it. What had just happened? Had I fallen asleep? I was suddenly dazed and bewildered. I jumped up from the chair, rubbing my eyes.

"You have a daughter, *monsieur*," the doctor announced. "*Compliments!*"

I stared in amazement at the writhing body of my daughter, the umbilical cord still linking her with her mother. As awed as I was to finally see my first child, I was still trying to get my bearings. What the hell had just happened?

Two hours later, Camille and I were alone with our daughter. Camille was exhausted and sore. As she described it, she felt like she had been run over by one truck while another truck drove through the most sensitive part of her body. I'm embarrassed to admit how selfish I was. I was not in any pain and all I wondered was how long our sex life would be on hold. Of course, I didn't verbalize this concern. Our daughter peacefully sucked on her mother's nipple, her tiny hand caressing the breast. The tranquility and quiet were shocking after the bedlam of the birth. Equally shocking was the responsibility that I noticed for the first time settling heavily on my shoulders. I, alone, would determine whether my little princess would live or die, flourish or starve.

Camille reached over and grabbed my hand. "We have a daughter," she said, her eyes aglow.

"It hasn't sunk in yet."

"Thank you, Eric. It helped me having you there."

I shook my head. "I'm sorry. I lost it at the end."

"What are you talking about? Your were right above me."

I frowned. "You're crazy. I was sitting down. I wasn't even holding your hand."

"But I saw you right above me."

I clenched my jaw. I couldn't figure out what had happened in the delivery room. Actually, I tried not to dwell on it. I decided to file it away as a fainting spell and dream. But, how the hell could Camille have experienced the same dream? Especially when she was awake? This was not a path I cared to explore. "I don't know what you're talking about."

"But, Eric, I felt your hand—"

"Enough!" The baby jumped. I lowered my voice. "We're both tired. I'm going home to get some sleep. You should try to sleep, too."

I closed the door behind me, but didn't shut it completely. I stood in the hallway for several minutes, waiting.

I didn't know what to expect from Camille. She was the youngest of three children and had never held an infant before. I wanted to make sure she wouldn't panic now that she was alone with our daughter for the first time. What I heard was not what I anticipated.

"It was because of you, wasn't it?" I heard Camille say. "You awakened your daddy's spirit. You're our little angel."

Part of me wanted to throw open the door and demand to know what she meant. But a much bigger part did not want the answer. I never raised what happened in the delivery room with her and she never again raised it with me. The next day, when she told me she had set aside the girl's name we had agreed upon, and chose instead "Angélique," I didn't ask why.

As I later learned, you can run from your shadow for a long time. It may never catch up with you. But if you're looking over your shoulder at your shadow while you're running, you never see the brick wall in front of you.

❁   ❁   ❁

Five years later, I hit the wall. The number of children had increased to four. That's right—four children in five years. And the answer to your next question is: Yes, the Pétris family is Catholic.

Angélique was big sister to three brothers. Despite the exponential increase in the size of our clan, our lives were remarkably the same. We had moved to a larger two-floor condo, but still lived within three blocks of Place Belle Cour in the heart of Lyon. I still worked at the *cabinet d'avocats* Prétis et DeLorier—the law firm that my father had created. We went to the same parish church, had the same friends, had the same arguments, told the same jokes, had the same sex—you get the idea. It was not that we were adverse to change. On the contrary, Camille and I had dreamed of the day when we could leave behind Lyon and the infernal taxes of the French government, go off to some island in the Caribbean Sea and live off of the royalties from my writing. I, like countless others, was a hopeful author. I had penned four novels in five years. I had also filled two desk drawers with preprinted rejection letters from agents and publishers in Paris, London and New York. My family loved my books, but the Pétris clan was not large enough to form a viable customer base. And with four children to feed, a mortgage to pay, a car lease and the primordial need to have the best dressed children in the region, there was simply no alternative but to wait for something to break with one of my books. "Break" was the operative word. Only it was not one of my books that broke; I did.

I slammed my hand down on the kitchen table. Forks, knives and glasses rattled and my four children jumped. "Damn it!" I yelled. "Is it too much to ask that you behave at dinner? Your manners are terrible. You're all a bunch of animals." My eyes fell on my oldest, five year-old Angélique. Her mischievous blue eyes twinkled beneath blond bangs. She struggled in vain to muffle a laugh.

I traced her eyes to my wife. Camille was smiling, not trying as hard as Angélique to control herself.

Once *Maman* burst into laughter, all three children burst like champagne corks.

My face reddened as the blood rushed to my head. "You're a lot of help."

She shrugged her shoulders and looked at me with pity. "Be cool, Eric."

I shook my head in disgust. "You may not care if our children are undisciplined little jerks like most of the kids in this town, but I won't accept it. And if you won't help me, at least, don't undermine me." I surveyed my offspring. Angélique was the ringleader of this band of rebels. In her five years, I could not remember those gorgeous blue eyes ever registering fear of me. That was the problem. Without fear, she would never obey me. And while my younger sons, Pierre, Marc and Cédric, were scared white anytime I raised my voice, Angélique held power over them at least equal to mine. I could not fathom the source of her authority nor could I understand why they followed her so loyally.

After dinner, the children went off to play while Camille and I did the dishes. It had been a nightly ritual since our wedding, interrupted only when I had an important soccer game to watch. Camille had brilliantly moved the television in the adjoining family room so that I could watch my game through the pass-through while standing at the sink.

"I don't know why you have so little patience with them," Camille said, wiping off the table. "You're not the one spending all day with them."

"It seems like I have. You tell me every little thing they do wrong as if I can do something about it from my desk. Besides, when I call you from the office I can't even hear you over the phone. Someone's crying or screaming or yelling, 'Maman, Maman, Maman!'"

"Don't worry. I won't call you anymore." She huffed. "Want to trade places for a day?"

I turned towards her. "Give me a week with them and they'd be a whole lot better behaved."

Camille's eyes narrowed. "You're a jerk!"

"I'm not saying you're not doing a good job," I quickly retreated. "It's not your fault that they don't fear you."

"I don't want them to *fear* me," she said with disgust. "I want them to love me."

I let loose an exaggerated sigh. "So, you're just going to let them do whatever they want?"

"You don't know what I do every day from eight until six." Her eyes began to sweat. "You don't know what it's like to not have ten minutes of peace and quiet. There are times when—" she lowered her voice and checked the family room to see if the children were there. "There are times when I find myself hating them." Her whisper trembled and the tears flowed. "Do you know how awful that feels?" She began sobbing. "But I don't hate them. I love them. That's why it hurts so much to see you treat them like animals."

I quickly dried my hands and reached to take her into my arms. She pushed me back. "Don't touch me."

Her face was pained in a way that worried me. "What's wrong?"

"Don't you love your children?"

"Of course, I do."

"It doesn't seem like it. All you do is yell at them."

"I'm trying to give them a little discipline."

"I haven't seen you get down on the floor and play with them. You don't read to Angélique. You don't play soccer with your sons. It seems like they're just pieces of furniture for you."

"That's not true. Last weekend, I played with Pierre and Marc."

"For what—two minutes? Two minutes in a whole week."

"That's nonsense. You don't see all the time I spend with them."

"I don't see you being loving with them. Pierre cowers every time you walk by."

I hoisted myself up onto the counter and crossed my arms. "That just means he's done something wrong."

Camille shook her head. "No. That means he thinks you're always mad at him and that he doesn't know when he's done something wrong and when he hasn't."

"That's crap." I looked away and smiled.

"What?"

I knew I shouldn't say what was running through my mind, but I couldn't help myself. It was a saying Camille's father had taught me. "Give a child a spanking. Even if you don't know what it's for, the child will."

Her face grew sadder. "What happened to the kid I used to know?"

"I haven't changed."

"Yes, you have. Don't you see how cold and bitter you are? You used to be so fun and wild."

"In case you haven't noticed," I yelled, pushing myself off the counter, "there's a roof over our heads I have to pay for." I pointed. "There's a refrigerator that has to be filled every day. We have bills that I have to think about. Sorry if I'm not as carefree as you'd like, but the fact is I have responsibilities. All five of you!"

Camille looked at me coldly and then, turned and walked out. I followed her, but when she headed upstairs, I veered towards the living room and plopped down in front of the television.

This was fairly typical. There had been a great deal of tension between us lately. And our arguments often centered around the children. It was February and winters in Lyon were not extremely cold, but they were gray. It was a suffocating, claustrophobic gray. There is no volume, no sense of space. I couldn't remember the last time I'd seen the sun. And without the sun, there is no life. I blamed our moods and the children's unruliness on cabin fever. Nevertheless, I had to admit that I was not as loving as I would have liked to be.

Sometimes, I was able to dismiss it as a necessary counterweight to Camille. She and Angélique acted like two sisters, not mother and daughter. And the boys! I'd hate to run into a tornado with the energy and destructive power of those three. As their father, it was my sworn duty to instill at least a modicum of discipline in their lives. But when my mind had run through the litany of reasons why I had to be the disciplinarian, something inside of me wondered why I felt so little emotion. Actually, "so little" is an understatement. I felt nothing. Sure, there was an affinity towards my children—but only because they were mine. I had been crazy about Camille since the day I saw her. She was absolutely gorgeous. Five foot—ten, blonde, blue eyes, the body of a model even after four children, people looked at her and I could hear their thoughts: *What the hell is she doing with him?*

But my so-called craziness for her was not something I felt in my gut. Other than the foreign sense of agape I had felt at Angélique's birth, nothing seemed to stir in my heart. I'm not talking about agape in terms of wonderment. I mean agape in the classical Greek sense—a spiritual love; something you feel inside that transcends the senses and everything you've ever experienced physically. To have only felt it once in my life—there was something very wrong with that. This was not a recent observation. I remember travelling with my parents when I was a child. Whether watching the sun set over the Atlantic or coming upon a vista high in the Alps, I noticed everyone else in my family reacting to the beauty. I knew in my head it was beautiful. I just didn't feel anything. At the same time, however, I had always taken great pride in my logical, calculating mind. I just wondered why my mind operated to the exclusion of my heart.

After my blood had cooled, I turned off the television and headed upstairs. I found Camille crouched outside Angélique's room. She silently motioned for me to be quiet.

I approached and listened.

Angélique was talking. I had heard her talking to her dolls on countless occasions, so I wondered why Camille was so captivated. I listened, too. Then, it hit me.

Angélique was answering unheard questions and asking questions without giving a response. When she played with her dolls, or even with Cédric, Angélique provided both sides of the dialogue.

"*Oui*," I heard Angélique say. "Pierre gets into a lot of trouble. But he's a nice boy. . . Yes. . . Marc seems sad a lot. Do you know why? . . . Doesn't he know that already? . . . Okay. . . I love you, too. Will you sleep next to me tonight? . . . Thanks. Good night."

Camille stood up and I followed her into Angélique's room.

"Whom were you talking to, *chérie*?" my wife asked.

Angélique immediately looked at me. "Nobody."

Camille gestured with her eyes for me to leave. I was not taking orders. "We heard you talking, Angélique. Now, whom were you talking to?"

She was stoically silent.

Camille gave me another look. This time, I obeyed. I never had been able to break through the ramparts of these two women when they allied forces.

Ten minutes later, my wife came into our bedroom, a look of wonder on her face.

"Well?"

"She said she was talking to her angel."

"Like an imaginary friend?"

"No. Her angel." Camille headed to the bathroom to change.

What next went through my mind was likely different than a lot of people. I did not engage in a debate with myself as to whether angels exist. I was raised Catholic and I was one of the few people without gray hair in a "Catholic" country who actually practiced. I took it on faith that angels exist. And I believed that each of us has a guardian angel to do what it can to help us without walking on the toes of our free will. What I wondered, however, was whether it was possible for a human being—someone dwelling on the planet earth—to communicate with a nonphysical spiritual entity. This sounds like a deep metaphysical discourse. In reality, it was simply: "I've never seen or talked to angels. How could Angélique?" My problem was that I could not dismiss my daughter's explanation as merely the progeny of a five year-old's active imagination. When I was thirteen, I was sitting outside with my brothers and sisters, two cousins and grandmother. We were all praying the Rosary for my uncle who was dying of cancer. Somewhere in the middle of the third decade, I gazed to the south— towards the part of Lyon where he lived. It was a dark and overcast night. That's why the light I saw rising in the sky caught my attention. It rose straight up and up and up. I watched it for thirty seconds until it finally was too high for my eyes to follow. Given the clouds that blanketed Lyon, there was no way I should have been able to see it—certainly not for so long. Without thinking, I knew what it was. My uncle had died and I had seen his soul going up to heaven.

Even at age thirteen, I realized that heaven was not some planet beyond the reach of our telescopes. But, I knew what I saw and what it represented.

I turned to my sister sitting next to me. She continued reciting her prayer and leaned closer.

"Eduard just died," I whispered.

She looked at me with a strange confidence. Ten seconds later, the phone rang in my grandparents' house. My grandfather opened the window. In a quivering voice he said, "Eduard has gone to heaven."

Lying in bed, thinking back to that night in April twenty years ago, I realized there was a profound difference between being *allowed* to see something supernatural like that and actually being *capable* of communicating with a spiritual being. I never again experienced anything like it. After my father died, I desperately wanted to see or talk to him. If I could see my uncle's soul take flight from his body, I figured I was entitled to some sign from my dad. But it was not to be. There were so many charlatans claiming to be able to communicate with the "spirit world" and ripping off desperate people. It was a huge industry in France. Throughout the world, probably. It had even invaded Camille's family. Her grandmother claimed to be clairvoyant. While I heard some interesting stories about her predictions, the "predictions" were all announced after the fact.

"Pretty amazing," Camille commented upon returning to the bedroom, dressed only in a tee-shirt. She dove under the covers.

"Not really," I responded facetiously. "Don't forget. She's your grandmother's great-granddaughter and they say the *gift* skips two generations."

Camille turned away in disgust and reached for her book.

"What do you make of it?" I asked more to make peace than out of curiosity.

She was giving me the silent treatment.

"Please."

Continued silence.

"I'm sorry about the grandmother crack. I really want to know if you believe she was talking to something."

"I do." Her tone was defiant.

"To an angel?"

"Sure. Why would she lie?"

"She doesn't have to lie. She just might not know the difference between reality and her imagination."

"Angélique?" asked Camille, her eyes challenging me.

She was right. Angélique not only had the attitude of a teenager, she also had the savvy and intelligence of someone much older than five. "But how—I mean, talking to angels!"

"Don't you believe in the apparitions at Lourdes? How about Fatima? Those were just ordinary children living on a farm."

"Exactly. Not *my* children."

"What about Pierre?"

"What about him?" I asked, nervous that she was going to tell me that, while I was at the office every day, my oldest son spent his time playing with tarot cards.

"Don't you remember what happened?"

A shrug communicated my ignorance.

"That night—" she pointed to the foot of our bed and then at the wall above our window. How I forgot that incident I don't know. As soon as Camille reminded me, the memory was as clear to me as anything that had happened within the previous twenty-four hours. Maybe, I simply chose to forget.

I had gotten home late from work. Camille was already in bed, as were Angélique and Marc. Cédric was not yet born. Pierre, however, had taken a long nap that afternoon and was keeping his mom company until dad got home, as was his rightful duty as the man of the house.

While I undid my tie, Camille filled me in on her day with the children. I never liked to talk about work. So, when she asked me what was new at the firm, I almost always said, "Nothing." That gave her the green light to tell me about the fortunes and misfortunes of the day in the Pétris asylum. It must have been about two or three minutes into this conversation when, suddenly, she stopped mid-sentence and her eyes locked on Pierre. He knelt at the foot of our bed, his hands clasped under his chin, and his eyes . . . I'd never seen such a look before. His eyes were wide, his smile wider. His face was absolutely radiant. He seemed to be in total rapture. After several seconds, I followed his line of sight across our bedroom to the wall above our windows. The curtains were drawn. I looked for a spider or some other creature since I knew all too well of his fondness for insects. There were none. The white wall was bare. But he clearly saw something.

My attention returned to Pierre. I noticed that he had yet to blink.

"Are you alright, Pierre?" Camille asked, sitting up and approaching our son.

"Pierre!" I called out loudly.

Not only did he not react, he still had yet to blink.

I walked closer and snapped my fingers in his line of sight.

No reaction.

I waved my hand three inches in front of his face. It was as though my hand were invisible to him. I snapped again. Again, no reaction.

Camille sensed that I was about to grab him by the shoulders. "Leave him alone," she said.

I crawled into bed next to her, still dressed in my dark blue suit. We watched him for several minutes. "What do you think he's looking at?" I finally asked.

Camille smiled. "Maybe, your dad."

The notion appealed to me. My father had died between our engagement and our wedding. He never knew any of his grandchildren.

Pierre suddenly turned towards us. His face was back to normal. He was blinking again. He still had a smile on his face, but then, Pierre was a natural grinner. His behavior did not suggest that anything even slightly out of the ordinary had just occurred.

"Hey, Pierre," I immediately said. "What were you looking at?"

He made some sounds, but Pierre could not yet talk. It had been a source of concern for Camille and me. He was almost two and I couldn't understand a damn thing the kid said.

Camille and I both peppered him with questions like reporters at a press conference. We never did learn what

it was that he saw. But there was no doubt in our minds—
he saw something that we could not see.

Camille was tired of arguing with me. She had concluded that Angélique really did see and speak with an
angel and left me to my own devices. She closed her book,
turned off the light and kissed me good-night. I tossed
and turned for several hours. Bedtime is either the best
or worst time of the day. There's no middle ground. You
either sleep the sleep of the just, as my dad used to say, or
your subconscious bombards you with thoughts from
which you can't defend yourself. There's nowhere to go,
nothing to do. The senses are turned off. The only thing
left operating is the mind. And the mind without dis-
traction is a frightening thing. I don't remember the ser-
pentine path along which my subconscious led me that
night. But I do remember its destination: I, Eric Pétris,
husband and father of four; provider, hunter for the clan;
king of the castle; was in spiritual day-care while my tod-
dlers were working on their doctorates.

❀   ❀   ❀

Spring finally arrived in Lyon. Every year, it was like watching a teeter-totter shift in weight from one side to the other. With each hike in the mercury, each additional ray of sunshine, the Lyonnais emptied the cafés' interiors and filled the tables on the sidewalks. The city was alive again. And there was something alive inside of me.

Epiphanies happen in different ways to different people. I've known some who have had that "Aha!" experience. I never have. Instead of turning the corner and bumping into Truth, I always walked by Truth without noticing her. Only hindsight allows me to retrace my footsteps, knock myself on the head, and say, "Of course! That's who that was."

After the discovery of Angélique's angelic conversations, I returned to the routine of the five-day workweek. Routine, whether it was at work, at home, or in school, had always been my security blanket. I would have liked to be more spontaneous, but, subconsciously, I craved the familiar. Lately, however, I found the routine extremely unsettling. Nothing in my life was improving. Despite my promotions and incumbent raises, we were in the same financial position as when we were first married. Neither Camille nor I was frivolous. We watched what we spent carefully. But every time we got a few months ahead, something would hit us out of the blue. It seemed inevitable. Pierre was two when we were travelling in the United States and he had to be hospitalized for viral pneumonia. The French social security agency covered only five percent of the hefty American medical tab. We've "loaned" money to Camille's family with no hope of ever being repaid. Vacations always cost more than budgeted. And then, there were all the little things—electronic devices like computers, cameras and televisions that died; extraordinary car repairs; home repairs. It all added up. If matters weren't improving financially, then, they must have been improving in other arenas, right? I looked. And what I discovered was complete stagnation.

Camille and I were no closer than when we were first married. If anything, we were more divided. I had read countless books, but was no more intelligent. I was no better a parent. Despite my concerted efforts at disciplining my children, they fought and cried and whined more than ever. Worse, after several spanking sessions, my conscience pointed out that it was my temper fueling the punishment, not love. And when my conscience failed to make itself heard, Camille spoke for it. Where the hell was all this leading? I asked myself this question each day in one form or another. I was becoming dangerously restless.

By the first week of April, my sister, Elisabeth, had moved back to Lyon and her boyfriend, Christophe, had followed her. There had been a rupture in their relationship and Christophe left everything behind in Nice to make a final attempt to win my sister's hand.

I realize that it's risky to casually apply labels to people, but, in this case, I know of what I speak. Elisabeth, as a child, was the Angélique of my family. She was sharp, rebellious, and constantly challenging our parents. She took nothing on my parents' word, demanding a full explanation for everything, and always testing the bounds of her territory. It is ironic that she was a quasi-hero to us as children, whereas, now, Angélique and I were on opposite teams. Had any of my other sisters brought home Christophe, we would have done our utmost to destroy the relationship in its infant stage. But since Elisabeth chose him, there was an unspoken, albeit unenthusiastic, acceptance. He was the antithesis of what we were. He had a ponytail and, God help him, an earring. A year into their courtship, we discovered he had added a tattoo and nipple ring. He was certainly not the prototype of the Pétris family member. Additionally, he was laid-back, relaxed and refused to criticize anyone or anything. He was simply too damn lukewarm. Or, so I thought.

Elisabeth and Christophe began coming to our place on weekends as the weather improved. We would sit out on our balcony for hours, talking, drinking beer or wine and smoking cigarettes. Sometimes, they joined us at Parc de la Tête d'Or, where we would play soccer with the children and picnic in the vast park. Throughout these get-togethers, Christophe remained strangely silent, or, he left us to play with my children. He was not shy. I assumed he was just uninterested in our conversations. We typically discussed those subjects that were taboo in the larger French society: religion, right and wrong, and personalities. The personalities we discussed were always ourselves, our brothers, sisters, and mother.

Elisabeth and Christophe had the irritating habit of showing up at our condo at least two hours later than the time promised. One Sunday in late May, after predicting an arrival time of one-thirty, they arrived at four-thirty. After depositing the wine and snacks they brought, they found me on the balcony.

"*Bonjour*, Eric," Elisabeth said, coming around the table to give me a kiss.

"You mean, '*Bon soir*,' don't you?"

"Good to see you, too," my sister laughed.

Christophe and I also exchanged the mandatory *bise*. "What's up?"

"I don't mind optimism, but it's not polite to tell us you'll be here at a certain time and then show up three hours later."

"Sorry," Elisabeth said. "We just lost track of time."

"Doing what?"

"We went up to Fourvière for mass at noon. The view was incredible. We ended up sitting on a bench overlooking the city and time seemed to stop."

I smiled sarcastically. "You sat on a bench for three hours?"

Elisabeth and Christophe looked at each other.

"What?"

"We tried a meditation together."

I rolled my eyes. These two were not only late for family gatherings, their births were two decades too late.

"It was really cool," Christophe said. "You might like it."

"Try to be one with the universe?" I asked sarcastically. "Thanks, but I'll pass. Besides, my prayers work just fine."

"I'm not saying you have to meditate, Eric, or even that you should," Elisabeth countered. "I can only speak for myself, but meditation has become an important part of my prayers. In fact, one of the reasons why our meditation was so amazing on Fourvière was because we just got out of mass."

"Whatever." I pushed myself out of my chair. "Anyone else want a *mousse*?" Christophe signaled for one and I headed inside for two beers. Upon my return, Camille had settled in and was talking to my sister and her boyfriend about their experience that afternoon on Fourvière.

"Eric, you should hear this," Camille commented.

"I really don't like all this New Age crap you're getting into, Elisabeth." I shot a glance at Christophe, the intent of which was to let him know I thought he was to blame for my sister's new interest.

My sister smiled at me, shaking her head. "You're not honestly worried about me becoming a heretic, are you?"

I gave a noncommittal shrug.

Camille dismissed me with a wave. "So, anyway, tell me what happened."

Turning my chair and propping my feet up on the balcony's railing, I feigned disinterest. The view from our condo was magnificent. We were on the fifth floor and the buildings in front of us were all smaller, giving us an only slightly obstructed view of the Saône River and Vieux Lyon. I tried to tune out Elisabeth's voice. My eyes followed a pigeon. It glided past us, then began to climb. After thirty seconds, I lost it over Fourvière. The sight of the hill brought me right back to the conversation I was trying to avoid.

". . . I wanted to know if it really worked," Elisabeth was saying. "So, I asked God to give me a sign. Then, after Communion, I concentrated on sending out white light to everyone in church—"

"White light?" I interrupted.

"Yes. Love, positive energy."

I crossed my arms and rolled my eyes.

"Ignore him," Camille ordered. "Go ahead."

"Then, as Christophe and I were leaving the basilica, he turned to me—" Elisabeth laughed. "I'm sorry. I'm so bad about speaking for you. You tell it."

"You're doing fine," Christophe said with an affectionate smile.

"So, he turned to me and said, 'That was incredible. It was the most amazing mass I've ever been to. After communion, I felt so much love I wanted to reach out and hug everyone.'"

I don't know how my face gave away my shock and disbelief. Even if I'd been trying not to show it, I couldn't have. Christophe looked at me and nodded, silently assuring me that it was true. It was difficult to believe he'd said that to Elisabeth. Christophe was not a churchgoer. And, when he did go, it was because Elisabeth dragged him kicking and screaming. The only reason he ever acquiesced was to appease her. I had heard, never directly from Christophe, that he thought mass was pointless, that it was a waste of an hour. So, for him to say that it was the most amazing mass he'd been to, at first blush, wasn't saying all that much. On the other hand, for him to admit getting anything, much less something "incredible," out of his time in church was earth-shattering.

"You got your sign," Camille concluded.

Elisabeth nodded emphatically. "Then, we decided to meditate together. We were sitting on the bench overlooking the city, but after a minute, we turned towards each other. We looked into each other's eyes and ... holy shit!"

"What?"

Elisabeth squinted, trying to find the words. "This is going to sound really bizarre. But, we were communicating without talking."

"You mean, telepathy?" I laughed.

"I don't know what you call it," Elisabeth said. "But we each went inside the other's head. Well, I shouldn't say that. I don't really know what happened, except that I knew what he was thinking and he knew what I was thinking. It scared the shit out of me at first."

"Me, too," Christophe chimed in.

"But, then, we just relaxed and went with it."

Camille's mouth was open and I was frowning. "You're screwing around in dangerous territory."

"How so?" asked Elisabeth.

"All this New Age crap is about eliminating right and wrong, eliminating God and making everybody into a god."

"There are pitfalls to everything," Elisabeth allowed, "but what I've experienced so far has brought me closer to God."

"If that's true," I asked, "then why were you scared when you started picking up on Christophe's thoughts?"

"Because I'm new to this," she admitted. "I don't always know what I'm doing. I try to filter."

"Filter?" asked Camille.

"Yeah. I try to figure out if what I'm doing is right, if what I'm experiencing is true. Basically, I try to check in with my conscience as much as possible. That's what I mean by 'filter.'"

"To each, his own," I said. "If you get something out of it, great. But that stuff isn't for me."

"It might be."

"How so?" I asked my sister.

"Have you asked yourself why none of your books has been published yet?"

I reeled. "What the hell does that have to do with anything?"

"One of the things I've realized is that, to a certain extent, we make our own reality," she explained. "If you're not yet a full-time author, maybe it's because you're sabotaging yourself."

"And where does God's will fit into all this?"

"What do you mean?"

I stretched out my arms. "If I'm the master of my own domain, if I can dictate the outcome, God's will is meaningless. My will replaces God's will. At least, according to you."

"Look," my sister said, frowning now. "I'm not an expert. I'm just throwing this out on the table. Take it or leave it. But I've been thinking a lot about you lately. It seems like everything I've read in the last month has reminded me of you and your dream to be a full-time writer. It could be that it's God's will that you're a full-time writer and that you're blocking it with limiting beliefs."

"Or," I said, moving in for the kill, "it could be that it's God's will that I *not* be a full-time writer and all the meditations, crystals, incense and New Age crap in the world won't change a thing."

"That's a cop-out!"

"No, the cop-out is resorting to your 'feel-good—I can do no wrong' philosophy."

"You think it's easy?" Elisabeth asked, her face reddening. "Try looking inside yourself, figuring out all the crap you're carrying around with you—the fears, the old, limiting beliefs. Face yourself and then tell me it's a cop-out."

Christophe put his arm around her.

Camille turned to me. "Listen to your sister. She's right."

"Don't tell me. You, too?"

"That's right. Me, too. In fact, instead of reading other people's thoughts, I feel their feelings. And, right now, you're scared to death, Eric."

I rolled my eyes. "Yeah, that I married a psycho."

"You can be such a jerk!"

"I don't see why I'm a jerk. I'm the only one here who has a full-time job. I'm the only one who has more than just my mouth to feed. I'm the only—"

"*Tais-toi!*" Camille ordered, her voice low and angry. "That's an excuse, too, Eric. You protect yourself with all your so-called responsibilities. But everything you talk about is on the outside. You should worry instead about what's on the inside."

I laughed sarcastically. "What I wouldn't give to have nothing to worry about but self-evaluation, to go off on my own for a year and *find myself.*"

A long period of silence ensued. It was finally broken when Angélique opened the balcony door and asked her mother for an Orangina.

"I'll get it," I offered, anxious to leave the discomfort of the balcony.

I made my way to the kitchen, my little girl leading the way. She opened the refrigerator, pulled out the pear shaped bottle and handed it to me. I heard the television in the family room blaring out the latest Disney video we had purchased. The day before, Pierre had spilled apple juice in the family room, staining the rug. As I reached for a glass, I decided to insist that Angélique drink the Orangina in the kitchen. She would protest, I knew, and I was preparing to stand my ground.

"Why do I have to drink it in the kitchen?" she demanded.

I turned in shock. Before my jaw dropped, the glass did. It shattered and exploded across the tile floor. "Don't move!" I yelled. She was barefoot, so, I hoisted her into my arms and carried her out of the kitchen.

"Why did you ask me that?" I asked after setting her down in the family room.

It was evident from her face that she was confused.

"Why did you ask me why you had to drink it in the kitchen?"

"Because I wanted to watch the movie," she replied.

"But I didn't tell you that you had to drink it in the kitchen."

She tilted her head as if to see whether I was really her father. "Yes, you did. I heard you."

At this point, my stomach dropped. I left her with her brothers and returned to the disaster area. Camille and Elisabeth had heard the glass break and met me in the kitchen.

"What happened?" asked my wife.

Elisabeth looked at me curiously. "Are you okay? You're pale."

"Um ... see ..." I scratched my head. "I don't know what just happened." I thought back to thirty seconds earlier. I knew I hadn't said a word. And yet, Angélique heard exactly what I was thinking. Coming on the heels of Elisabeth's story, Angélique's words were chilling. Then, I thought about what Camille had said about feeling other people's feelings. Strangely, it made perfect sense. I had never known anyone who could talk on the phone with her parents, brother or sister for an hour, hang up, and then never be able to recount more than five seconds of conversation. It used to make me mad. I thought she was keeping something from me. But, no matter how irritated I became, she just squinted, shrugged and said, "I can't remember anything except that my dad was extremely depressed."

"Why?" I would ask. "What did he say?"

"I just got that sense."

As if on cue, a shudder ran up my spine. I was surrounded by people with apparently paranormal gifts or powers. After chewing on that thought a second, I realized that maybe, it was I who was abnormal.

I recounted what occurred to my wife and sister. Camille went in search of Angélique while Elisabeth helped me clean up the glass.

"Are you having trouble deciding what happened?" she asked after a moment.

I didn't respond. I was in a free-fall. My stomach was in knots. What the hell was happening to my quiet, sedate life? I could handle trouble at work—even getting fired, no matter how remote the possibility at *Pétris et DeLorier*. With all of the privatization of government-owned companies and the new need to answer to shareholders, "downsizing" had recently been introduced into the French vocabulary and the newspapers were full of sob stories. But my home life was supposed to be the eye of the storm—the place where peace reigned despite the tempest surrounding us.

I looked up at Elisabeth. Her smile suggested that she vicariously felt my pain. I quickly turned away. After vacuuming the floor, I returned to the balcony. It was evident that Elisabeth had explained to Christophe what had happened.

"Do you want to talk about it?" she asked.

I nodded.

"What do you think happened?"

"I don't know."

Elisabeth laughed. "That's the first time, I think, I've ever heard you admit that."

"How did she—I mean, did she really hear my thoughts so clearly that she thought I was talking? Is that possible?"

Elisabeth lit a cigarette. "Possible? I believe most young children are born with spiritual gifts that allow them to see and hear things that we, as adults, no longer can. But whether *I* think it's possible or not doesn't matter."

"But why?" I asked. "What's the point of allowing a child the ability, but not adults?"

"What if it's not taken away from adults?" asked Elisabeth. "Maybe, children reach a certain age, and, in order to conform to those around them, consciously or subconsciously, just reject their abilities. There's a lot of pressure not to be different."

"This is too much to swallow at once."

Camille arrived on the balcony. "Angélique thought she heard you say she had to drink in the kitchen."

"I know. But I didn't say a word. I swear. That's what I was thinking, though."

"It's pretty cool," Elisabeth said with a smile.

"She's special," Camille commented.

"Your children blow my mind," said Christophe.

"He speaks!"

Christophe shrugged.

"Why are you always so quiet?" I asked.

He shrugged again.

"I'm serious. You never get involved in any of our conversations. You manage to sit here for hours without saying anything. Are you bored?"

Christophe shifted uncomfortably in his chair. "It's not that I'm bored. It's just that ..."

"What?"

"Go ahead and tell him," Elisabeth said.

Christophe was playing with his ponytail. "I find these conversations interesting but ... but a lot of the time, the points of view are so, you know, linear. Do you know what I mean?"

"I don't have the first clue."

He held up his hands in front of his face, both palms flat and facing down. "It's like you guys talk about a subject. And, you know, everyone has his or her point of view. But you're all coming at the subject from the same plane," he said, moving his hands horizontally around the invisible subject suspended in midair. "I'm quiet because I'm trying to picture the subject on a nonlinear level."

"As in three dimensional?" I asked.

He nodded. "Yeah." He began circling his hands around the invisible subject, moving vertically in different directions. "I'm trying to see how the subject looks from on top and from underneath, not just the sides."

I had no idea what he was saying. Strangely, though, it rang true. If just about anyone else had told me what Christophe just told me, I'd have been irritated and taken it as an insult. But, one thing I had to admit about Christophe, he was honest and non-judgmental to a fault.

It was a commentary, not a criticism. "What do you make of what happened to Angélique?" I asked him.

Camille raised her hand to add to the question. "And what do you make of what happened between you and Elisabeth on Fourvière?"

"I think," Christophe said, "that all these things happened today for a reason. It's really easy to miss the strings that link seemingly unrelated occurrences together. This is a good example. I think that what Elisabeth and I experienced on Fourvière was a gift with two purposes. To let us know what's out there—what the possibilities are. I don't think I could do that again right now if I tried. So, it's something to shoot for. Also, what happened gives a whole lot of support to what Angélique did. She registered your thoughts just like Elisabeth and I registered each other's."

"But why did both happen today?" I asked.

Christophe smiled at me. "You're the only one who can answer that question."

"What do you mean?"

"It seems pretty obvious that, since it was your thoughts that Angélique read, that experience was meant for you. I don't know why. Only you do."

WHY? It had been my favorite question as a child and, especially, while studying philosophy at the university. But, once my first child could speak, it became the question I despised most. "I don't know," I said weakly.

"Yes, you do," my wife said.

"I don't. If you know, tell me."

Camille leaned forward. "If Elisabeth, Christophe and I had the answers to every one of your questions, don't you think we'd tell you? There's a reason we don't have them. The answers are inside of you. You just have to have the courage to find it."

It is very difficult to describe what I was feeling at that point. It seemed as though a series of levees built around me were collapsing, one after another. I was being flooded. By what? I didn't know. Emotion? Truth? Childhood experiences? Whatever it was did not wait for me to identify it. It was coming fast and with a ferocity that paralyzed me. I couldn't stop it, but then, again, I didn't want to. "How?"

"Why don't you try meditating," Christophe suggested. "A lot of clarity can come from that."

Just minutes earlier, I was playing the teenaged brat, too cool and too intelligent to be interested in the conversation about meditation. Now, I was silent. Silent, but rapt.

"Do you want to do one now?" asked Camille.

"Not right now." I was going to offer an excuse, but realized it was futile. The bottom line was that I was

scared. I didn't know why. I just was. And the three of
them knew it.

Elisabeth explained to me how she meditated should
I ever choose to give it a try. I listened closely. But I had
no intention of actually making use of her instructions.
The water level was rising. I knew I didn't have much
time to get to high ground. The only thing nearby was a
tower, but I was afraid of the boogey-man that I had, as a
child, heard lived there.

Camille put her hand on my knee. "Ask the Holy
Spirit for guidance and wisdom," she advised. "I always
get an answer."

Without thinking, I did just that.

You've heard the cliche, I'm sure—be careful what
you ask for; you just might get it. This was one of those
occasions where, had I known what I was getting, I would
not have asked.

For the balance of the evening, I was a zombie. At
least, that's how it must have seemed to them. They continued talking. Camille talked about our desire to leave
Lyon and make a new life in the Caribbean. Christophe
and Elisabeth thought it was a great idea. They discussed
the children some more. And they discussed some of the
things Elisabeth had discovered about herself. I heard
bits and pieces. And, although I appeared catatonic, I was
erupting inside. All my protesting and *ad hominem* at-

tacks aside, everything Christophe, Camille and Elisabeth had said stuck to me. That's the strange thing about truth. You can shun it, disparage it, bury it, even kill it. But, like a murder victim, it will always leave traces of its blood on you. Unseen, infinitesimal traces that haunt you until, when you are finally put under the microscope of your conscience, justice is done.

❦　　　❦　　　❦

I was a no-show at work the next three days. I was in the office, but I accomplished next to nothing. I couldn't eat, sleep or concentrate on anything except what was happening inside of me. There was a church three blocks from my office. It was where I went to mass when holy days of obligation fell during the week. Over the course of those three days, I visited that church more than ten times.

When my father died, he was on life-support for thirty-six hours. His heart ventricle fibrillated, meaning that, instead of pumping blood, there was an electrical short and the heart went into a sort of spasm. The fibrillation continued for twenty-five minutes. Five minutes without blood flow is fatal; or, if not fatal, results in permanent and massive brain damage. At some level, we knew that he was never again going to open his eyes. But God was kind enough to allow us the time to accept the fact that our father was gone. That did not stop me from praying from the depths of my soul for a miracle. I prayed and prayed until I sobbed. They were the most fervent prayers I had ever offered. It was the only time I had cried since age eight. After thirty-five hours, the physician announced the result of the brain scan. Only the lower stem of my dad's brain—the part that controlled his heart—functioned. Without a debate, my mother acquiesced to having the respirator removed. Only thirteen minutes later, with no physical reaction from his body whatsoever, he flat-lined.

My visits to the church around the corner from my office exceeded my prayers at my father's bedside in both fervor and desperation. Hunched over a pew, shaking, and cold, I begged God to help me. I didn't care what I had to face. I just knew I couldn't go on with this turmoil inside me. I was ready to face whatever was causing it.

I did not return time after time to church merely out of habit, or because I was programmed from my youth to seek my answers there. Every time I sat in church, my prayers were answered. I was either given strength to continue, or, a portion of the veil was pulled away. What the lowering of the veil revealed were events from my childhood and adolescence. I was happy for any insight, but I didn't know what to do with the information. For example, I remembered coming home one morning after having gone into town with my father for coffee and croissants. My paternal grandfather was there, tool box at his side, unlit cigar in his mouth, waiting for me. He and my grandmother lived in a *dépendance* on our property in the suburbs of Lyon. Whether out of a sense of obligation since he wasn't paying rent to my parents, or, out of a desire to teach me how to be a handyman, he was constantly appropriating my services to make repairs and improvements to the house and grounds. The morning I remembered was interchangeable with dozens of other Saturday and Sunday mornings over the course of many summers.

I turned to my dad as the car slowed, waiting for the garage door to open. "Please, dad, don't make me help Papet today."

My dad just laughed.

It was not the most pleasant memory of my childhood, but it certainly was not traumatic. In fact, since owning my own residence, I had been shocked at how much I learned and retained from my grandfather's lessons and had offered a silent prayer of thanks to him countless times. So, why was this memory coming to me in church? How was it the answer to what was happening to me?

Wednesday night, I was desperate for answers. I was going to resort to meditation. I recalled Elisabeth's instructions. At the time, I thought doing a meditation was like putting together a child's toy—there's a right way and a wrong way. Follow the directions and your child will smile. Fail to follow the directions and you're better off throwing away the pieces before your child realizes what you've done.

After Camille and the children were in bed, I went into our living room, turned off the lights and sat on the couch.

I took a deep breath, held it for a second, then, slowly exhaled. I repeated this several times over the next five minutes. The effect of simply breathing deeply was astounding. I immediately felt a peace wash over me. Then, I asked my guardian angel to wrap his wings around me for protection. I imagined opening the top of my head and summoned the white light of God's love and grace.

I imagined it filling my entire body. The sensation was a strong one and I opened my eyes. I saw silver sparkles all around me. I recognized those silver sparkles, that shimmering light. When I stood in front of Camille in church, the day of our wedding, our four hands connected, I saw the same silver sparkles. In fact, the cloud of shimmering light that surrounded us blocked out everyone else in church. I didn't just have the impression that we were standing on the altar in an empty church, I couldn't see anyone or anything else. Like so many times when the spiritual rose to the surface, my mind dismissed the experience as the progeny of nerves, light-headedness, or emotion.

This time, however, I knew it was real. Trusting in my angel's protection, I asked that God show me what was happening in my life.

The vision of that weekend morning and my grandfather waiting for me returned. It was vivid. But what did the memory mean tonight?

"How did you feel?"

That was the question posed to me. I can't say that it wasn't conjured by my imagination. It certainly wasn't asked by a voice outside of me. But, the question was not one I had entertained until that moment.

"Well, I felt—what difference does it make how I felt when I was ten years old?"

"How did you feel?"

"Answer my question first," I insisted.

This time, there was a distinct voice I heard. It was not my own. "How did you feel?"

I was immediately frightened by the intrusion of the foreign voice. I had, at first, engaged in a silent debate as to whether I was the source of the question, or, whether my mind was simply an antenna catching a signal. Now, there was no doubt. And without room for doubt, my comfort level drooped like an undercooked souffle.

"I felt trapped, like I had no choice."

"And?"

"I didn't like being unable to decide what to do and what not to do."

"What you like or don't like is irrelevant. How did you *feel?*"

"I felt powerless—powerless to choose. I didn't want to spend the entire day doing chores with my grandfather, but I was powerless to refuse."

"How did you feel when your dad laughed?"

"I didn't like it."

"I just told you that—"

"Sorry," I hurried to say. "I felt abandoned. He knew what it was like. He'd gotten roped into doing chores when he was my age. I was hurt that he didn't stand up for me."

"Good."

I was confused. My insides were churning faster than before, but I was no closer to understanding what this forgotten incident meant.

"So, what's the point?"

I received no verbal response. Instead, I felt the same powerlessness, the same hurt that I experienced when I was ten. The feelings were real—they were actual. It was like I was transported back in time. When they subsided, I was struck by another memory.

I was in my early teens and our family was vacationing at a hotel on the Côte d'Azur. There were three tennis courts, a pool, and, of course, the beach. My brother and I would spend most of the day at the tennis courts, heading to the beach for a swim when the courts filled. What struck me was the amount of time we spent waiting to get a court of our own, or to be invited to play with adults. That was it. We had been told by our parents that, being children, we had to vacate a court as soon as any adults showed up to play, regardless of whether we were there first. And, for that reason, we were not allowed to reserve court times. At the same hotel, I remembered staying up late with my parents, sitting with them in the lobby, listening to their conversations and debates with other guests. It was made clear to me that I was allowed to stay up as long as I realized my status—

child among adults. I, therefore, kept my mouth shut and was praised for doing so.

"And?"

"How did you feel?"

"It didn't really matter to me. As long as Thomas and I could play tennis, we were in seventh heaven."

"How about the late night conversations in the lobby? How did you feel about not being able to say anything?"

"Again, I didn't care. I was just happy to be a spectator." I laughed. "Those were the days. I wish I'd never grown up."

"Tell me about the people with whom your parents were speaking."

"There were all different kinds of people. They were guests at the hotel. Some were nice, some not. Some were smart, some not. What does it matter?"

"Digest it."

"Digest what?"

I knew it was over. I tried to make it continue, but the veil was not going to be lifted anymore tonight. I immediately picked up the phone and called Elisabeth.

After telling her what happened, she excitedly asked me, "So, what do those memories mean?"

"That's why I called you. I thought you could tell me."

"It seems that you have yet to deal with your feelings from the time you had to work with Papet."

"It's not like it was a big deal. I'd probably make my own sons do the same if dad was still alive."

"Knowing the feelings you had, you'd do the same to your sons?" she asked incredulously.

I hesitated. "Probably not. I make them help me do chores around the house, though."

She sighed. "I wonder if this has to do with how you treat your sons."

"In what way?"

"Well," Elisabeth said, "maybe your making them do certain chores bothers you because of how you felt when Dad made you help Papet."

I don't know how I knew, but it just didn't strike me. "That's not it."

"Why not?"

"It's different. I don't make them help someone else. Dad made me help Papet. It's different."

"How?"

I moved the receiver from my right hand to my left. "Dad could make me do whatever he wanted. But Papet couldn't. Not unless Dad told me take orders from Papet."

"That's it!" Elisabeth said excitedly. "You have to take back your power."

"Take back what—what are you talking about?"

"You just said it. The only reason that memory stuck with you is because you lost something there. If you felt powerless, then that's what you have to take back—power."

"But Dad didn't do anything wrong."

"It's not about blaming someone, Eric. This has nothing to do with Dad or Papet. It has to do with you. See, what you felt is what you felt. Neither right nor wrong. But now, you have to reclaim your power that you gave up to Dad and Papet."

I was willing to try anything. Besides, what Elisabeth said was stirring something in my gut. "How?"

"Try another meditation. See yourself taking back your power. Reach out, lovingly, and take it back. Thank them for holding it for you. And, then, take it back."

"Okay."

"That's it."

"Really? All I have to do is imagine myself taking it back?"

Elisabeth chuckled. "Eric, the hard part is facing the memory, realizing what it means, and experiencing the same feeling all over again. Once you've done that, the battle is ninety-nine percent won."

I hung up the phone and started another meditation. This time, once the white light began pouring down from heaven into me, I asked my guardian angel to carry me up to the source. I imagined my father and grandfather. While their images were certainly created by me, their presence was not conjured. I felt them with me.

My father smiled. My grandfather was expressionless. It troubled me. Why wasn't he happy with me? I extended my hand, waiting for them to return to me my power. My father obliged, beaming the pride of a father for his son. I turned to my grandfather, my hand still extended. He crossed his arms.

Elisabeth had said nothing about this.

"Give me back my power, Papet," I demanded.

He said nothing. He just stood there, his arms crossed, his face placid.

"I'm sorry, Papet, but I need to take this back."

Papet's look became stern.

I looked to my dad. He seemed oblivious to the fact that his father was making this hard on me.

"Papet, why won't you give me back my power?"

He did not respond.

Unlike my father, Papet was never an enigma. My father could be difficult to follow. I often wondered what was right and what was wrong in his eyes—much the same way Pierre wasn't sure how I'd react in any given situation. But Papet was easy to read. He had a ferocious growl, but was a kitten inside. He worried about my siblings and me. Growing up with a silver spoon in our mouths, he feared we would be too soft to survive adulthood. It was for that reason that he had insisted that I aid him in doing "manly" chores around our house.

Of course! It was the same lesson all over again. His crossed arms, his cold veneer. He was still trying to toughen me. And my apologizing was not exactly in keeping with the retrieval of my power.

I smiled at him. He didn't return my smile. But I knew it was a show. I kissed him on his cheek, then took his hands, uncrossed his arms, and pulled them towards me.

"I'm taking back my power, Papet. No apology. It's mine."

He didn't smile. It wasn't his style. The salute he gave me said it all.

I thanked them both for making their presence felt. I also thanked God and my guardian angel, then opened my eyes.

I was energized. I felt like I could climb Everest, swim *La Manche*—I could do anything.

Climbing into bed, I was careful not to disturb the slumber of Camille. I was surprised that none of our bedbugs had crept into our room. It had been months since one of the children had not climbed into our bed before midnight.

I closed my eyes. I wasn't at all tired. But it was late and I had to get up for work in the morning. It didn't matter. I was flying—literally and figuratively.

I had always believed that we had a soul. I knew that our soul was spirit, not a physical thing. After all, if we were really created in God's image, we could not be only physical beings. But I also assumed that our soul was trapped inside our bodies and just floated around until death, when it was finally liberated, and, either punished or rewarded dependent upon the actions of our physical body. The realization that we had the potential of engaging our souls—actually, that we had the *obligation* of developing our spiritual life—was exciting.

I had concentrated my studies in philosophy—particularly metaphysics and theology. My religious education was rigorous and I could debate any seminarian on Thomistic and Augustinian philosophies. In fact, while I was at the University, my comments after one Sunday mass caused the local priest to seek me out at my apartment to finish the debate. The debate lasted for three years. Friends and family had always come to me with questions about Catholicism, God, and sundry other philosophical topics. There had never been a question I couldn't answer.

Despite my learned background, however, there had always been something missing. It was not faith. Where logic stopped, I didn't. I believed in the tenets of Catholicism that could not be proven, such as the Trinity and Holy Eucharist. The trouble was that I didn't feel anything. All the religion was in my head, not my heart. As a young child, I would look around in church and note everybody's expressions. There were countless parishioners like me who had that "thousand-yard stare," obviously thinking about what they were going to do after mass let out. But there were those who were completely into the mass—both in mind and body. They felt something. How many times had I heard fellow Catholics complain that they got nothing out of going to mass? I could have said the same, but didn't. I took it on faith that the grace I received, even though I didn't feel it, served me. But I desperately wanted to *feel* it, too.

Lying in bed, after the meditation and my trips to church over the last three days, I smiled. I was finally feeling it. For more than thirty years I had operated under the assumption that it was enough to simply follow the rituals of my faith, to believe and to seek knowledge. I had been practicing religion. I had not been practicing spirituality. While my faith often spoke of the soul, I had never engaged my soul. So much of what I believed instantly took on a deeper, truer meaning.

With this realization came a strange sensation. I felt light and airy. The bed seemed to be swaying beneath me, as if I was on a boat, rocked back and forth from wave to wave. Then, the rocking stopped. I was floating. I looked down and saw my body, still in bed, lying on my stomach.

I wasn't scared. In fact, it seemed like the most natural thing in the world.

I decided that floating wasn't enough. I wanted to fly.

Instantly, I was over water.

A vast ocean spread below me in all directions. There was no land in sight. I flew just above the white caps, the salty wind moistening my face and blowing my hair. The sun shone brightly beyond scattered puffs of pure white clouds. Adjusting my arms, I changed altitude. I began climbing. Then, I descended. The speed was incredible.

I climbed a hundred feet, topped off and dove back to within a few feet of the sea. My stomach had the same giddy feeling as when I was a child on a roller coaster. I repeated the same movements for several minutes, following the same rhythmic ups and downs of an oscilloscope.

From just above the water, I pulled up. But this time, I did not stop. I climbed and climbed, not losing any speed. I targeted a cloud. I flew through it and climbed higher. There was no end to the sky. Instead of getting darker, the higher altitudes were whiter, clearer.

I evened out, pitched over, and shot back towards the water.

This time, I did not pull up.

I dove into the ocean like a bullet, cut through the water effortlessly, never losing velocity. I descended several hundred feet before reversing direction. I exploded out of the water, climbed and, then, dove back to the ocean. I reveled in this experience for ... well, I don't know how long it lasted. I've learned that in the non-physical world, time is meaningless. But, it seemed to last for over an hour.

I was ready to stop. And with that intention voiced inside me, it did stop. But, not for long.

A short time later, as I lay smiling on my pillow, I felt my spirit drifting again. *Okay*, I thought. *Let's go for another ride.*

This time, however, there was no sky, no ocean, no sun.

It was dark. I had trouble focusing on my surroundings in the blackness. I heard strange sounds. It took me several minutes to recognize the gnashing of teeth, growling and bestial cries. Everything, unfortunately, was coming into focus.

I was in the dungeon of a medieval castle. In front of me was an enormous jail cell with a gate that was four meters wide. Inside the cell were dozens of demons.

Instead of feet, they had hooves; yet they walked upright. Stubby, chipped horns rose out of their hairy heads. Their skin was red and, in some parts, scorched black. They were writhing in fury. Foam erupted from their fanged mouths. Their clawed hands gripped the enormous gate and shook it violently.

Their black, lifeless eyes were all on me.

I looked at the hinges of the gate. They were holding, but one of the demons had broken off another's finger and was using the dismembered finger to pick the lock.

At my side appeared six monks, dressed in brown robes and sandals. Their arms were crossed, their faces white with fear. They looked to me expectantly.

A crash echoed off the sweating stone walls. The demons had opened the gate to their cell. I rushed forward to stop their escape. Grabbing hold of the bars, I pushed the gate back. I was overpowering the demons, but they began scratching and biting at my hands. I couldn't stand the pain. My skin was split open, the demons' acidic saliva mixing with my blood.

I turned my head to ask the monks for help. One of them picked up a large wooden cross. I planted my foot on the ground to hold the gate in place and turned to catch the cross. I gripped the cross and pushed it against the bars of the gate. It crushed the hands of the demons and protected mine from their teeth and claws.

With a thrust, they fell back and I closed the gate. After locking it, I told one of the monks to stay and keep watch. I led the other monks up the cold stone stairs.

We found ourselves in a vast hall. There were no candles. Instead, the hall was illuminated by a supernatural storm whose flashes shone through long leaded glass windows. The monks followed me to the corner. There, we knelt before an altar and a picture of the Sacred Heart.

A small child stood on the altar, dressed only in a white robe. He was no more than two years old with curly blond hair and blue eyes. A halo of sparkling white spun above his head. My first reaction was that it was Christ. But Christ didn't have blond hair and blue eyes. As a child, I did. But, then again, I wouldn't have been sporting a halo.

I knelt there for several minutes without saying a word, the monks invisible behind me. I stared into the little boy's eyes and he returned my gaze. Neither of us smiled. Neither of us blinked. Time seemed frozen.

A rip of lightening shook the castle. I turned to look outside. The sky was full of flying demons now. They were assailing the castle.

The monk down in the dungeon screamed. "Help! Help! They're getting—"

An awful crash silenced him.

The growls and hissing of the demons grew louder, rising up the stairs. Their shadows were projected by the dungeon's torches on the enormous hall's walls. The remaining monks had fled.

I turned back to the little boy. "Protect me."

He shook his head. "No. It is you who must protect *me*."

"But, I can't. I'm only human. And ... and there are so many of them."

"You can do it. You must."

They reached the hall. I turned my back to the child and spread my arms to shield him. The demons approached slowly. They were hunched over, drooling, and baring their teeth. They numbered more than fifty. The demon leading them was taller and stronger than the rest. His face was just as grotesque as the others, but he seemed less like an animal. He did not salivate. He stood more upright.

It was Lucifer, himself, I realized.

He heard my thoughts and smiled proudly at being recognized. "Stand aside," he said in a surprisingly mellow, sophisticated voice.

"No."

He tilted his head left, then, right. The demons behind him spread out and formed a barrier, blocking the child and me in the corner. Slowly, they began closing in.

"What do I do?" I yelled to the child.

"Defeat them."

"But, I can't. That's Lucifer."

"So?" the child responded. "Don't you realize that love vanquishes evil?"

"There are too many of them."

"You are wrong," the child whispered. "Lucifer is alone."

I turned my head slightly. "Don't you see the other demons?"

"I see them, but they do not take orders from Lucifer. They take orders from you."

They were no more than three meters from me now.

"What do you mean?" I asked in desperation.

"The demons are your fears. Face them. Vanquish them. Eliminate them."

I closed my eyes tightly.

"The child is wrong," I heard Lucifer say in a calm, melodic voice. "Run. Get away while you still can."

Be gone, I thought, ordering my fears to depart. *Be gone. I order you!*

I opened my eyes. Every demon was still there, closing in. Lucifer cackled.

His eyes turned red and his mouth transformed from smile to snarl. "Get him!" he yelled.

I escaped back to my bed. I was sweating. My heart was pounding. I reached over and touched Camille to reassure myself that I was in our cozy condo in Lyon and not some supernatural medieval castle.

I was given no more than five seconds of respite. I knew it was not a dream, that I had been just as conscious as I was now. With that realization, the demons returned.

They were flying at me, one by one. I tried to return to my bed, but I couldn't. I was suspended in midair, facing off against winged demons. I was horrified. I was terrified. But, somehow, I was surviving. I kicked the first. I punched the second. I ducked as a third flew by, then, leveled an elbow into the face of the fourth. I was winning. But there was no end to the demons. Each one I defeated was replaced by another.

I jumped out of bed and ran downstairs. I tried dialing Elisabeth's number. But, my hand shook too much and I mis-dialed three times.

"Hello?"

"Oh, thank God, you're there, Elisabeth."

"Eric? I just got off the phone with you ten minutes ago. Where'd you think I'd be?"

I didn't even contemplate her words. What had been only ten minutes seemed like half a day to me. "I need your help."

"What's wrong?"

I quickly explained to her my visions. All the while, my body was shaking violently. I was cold, but sweating.

"Did you get grounded before your meditations?" she finally asked.

"Grounded? What's that?"

"I explained to you on Sunday."

"I wasn't paying that much attention," I admitted. "What do I do?"

She explained that I had to get *grounded.* "Imagine roots extending down through your legs, through your feet, and into the earth. The roots will go down to the core of the earth and around and around so that nothing can move you. Then, imagine the earth's energy rising up through the roots to you, then, filling your body with its warm amber-honey colored gel."

"Okay, thanks," I said quickly, ready to hang up and try it.

"Wait," her voice called out.

"What?"

"Eric, it's not about following certain directions or rituals." Her voice suggested her surprise at my childish approach.

"But I thought all that crap with the demons and Lucifer happened because I wasn't grounded."

I could hear her smile. "Grounding yourself just symbolizes your stability and your link to the earth. But you choose what to perceive in a meditation and you choose what to perceive in a dream. Think about it. The monks were probably just as you've always imagined them since you were a child. And the demons you described were probably stereotypes of evil that *you* conjured. All of that came from inside you."

"No way. I could never have imagined all I saw."

"Maybe not in a conscious state; at least, not if you tried. But in your meditation, you let go of the control and let your imagination bring it all to you. Just remember that your imagination is yours. You control it."

"But I couldn't control the demons. Definitely not Lucifer."

Elisabeth silently searched for a response. After twenty seconds, she said, "Remember when you were in high school and you kept having that dream about getting pushed off the cliff?"

"Yeah, night after night."

"What happened?"

The light bulb went on in my head. "I got it. One night, when I had that dream again, I finally willed, or, imagined, or, whatever—the guy that was pushing me to miss me and fall off the cliff without me. I'm supposed to dictate how the meditation unfolds."

"Not just in your meditations!" Elisabeth said excitedly. "In your life. In reality."

Five minutes later, I was sitting on the floor of my condo, begging my guardian angel to protect me. I had no idea what Elisabeth meant by her last comment—that I could will things to happen in real life like I did in my dreams. She often came out of the left field. In any case, I had more important things to worry about. Like Lucifer and his legions. I asked that my guardian angel summon his comrades, and, in case Lucifer came back, Archangel Michael as well. It was probably angelic overkill, but I wasn't taking any more chances tonight.

I engaged in the rooting or grounding exercise Elisabeth had suggested. After it was over, I rolled onto my stomach to fall asleep. "Please, guardian angel, protect me," I prayed silently.

Then, without expecting it, I received my angel's response.

I sensed he was spreading his wings and felt his weight as he laid down on top of me. I felt a feather tickle my cheek.

My imagination run amok? Or, as Elisabeth suggested, something I willed my imagination to conjure?

The level of reality of everything that had occurred that night seemed to negate such a conclusion. And, if my inner knowledge were not enough, my angel gave me proof. I reached over to set my alarm clock. I felt the same tickle again, this time on my neck.

A soft metallic sound came from the floor next to my bed. In the light that shined through the bedroom window, I saw on the floor the cross I wore. I grabbed for the chain around my neck. It was still there, intact, and unopened. Naturally, I assumed that the metal ring on the cross, through which passed the chain, had opened. I took the cross into the bathroom and turned on the light. The metal ring was not only unopened, but it was soldered closed. There was no possible way for the cross to have been disengaged from the chain. At least, no physically possible way.

I returned to bed feeling warm, protected and loved.

"What's wrong?" Camille asked without opening her eyes.

"Absolutely nothing, *ma chérie*. Go back to sleep."

I clenched the cross in my hand.

A chill ran up my spine and became a tear that fell from my eye. It was not a chill of fright. It was not a tear of sadness. It was the sense of agape that I had first experienced at Angélique's birth. I knew there was no denying tonight's experiences as I had denied what happened at her birth. I knew there was no turning back. Most important, I didn't want to retreat.

"I love you," I said to my angel. "And, thank you."

Another tickle, this time on my ear, was his response.

❁   ❁   ❁

"Do you talk to angels?" I asked Angélique. It was a question I would not have contemplated asking her less than a week earlier. But, now, I knew I had some making-up to do. I had to let her know it wasn't only alright for her to talk to her angel, but necessary and natural.

She looked at me with a mixture of confusion and concern.

When I asked her to come and sit with me on our balcony, I had expected her to immediately open up to me. I was stupid. For her entire life, I had been the speed bump that she'd come upon so often while cruising at five hundred kilometers per hour down the spiritual *autoroute*. She couldn't fathom a sudden change in my attitude.

"It's okay, *chérie*," I assured her. "You can tell me."

But, it wasn't okay with her.

"Do you want to color with me?"

I was frustrated. I wanted to drink from her well of wisdom. First, though, I had to prove myself worthy. How many times had Camille told me to be more patient with the children? Now, I had no choice. I couldn't make her talk. I couldn't make her trust me. She was in charge.

"Sure."

She ran inside to get her coloring book and colored pencils.

It had been two weeks since my showdown with the demons and Lucifer. I had learned my lesson about getting grounded at the outset of all meditations. As a consequence, I faced my demons now on my terms and not via out-of-body experiences. While I backed-down that night, I had made daily progress in eliminating the demons. I knew when one was lurking in the shadows. I was listening more to my intuition and to my body. I would become restless and would feel something brewing inside of me. Either in the sanctuary of church, or, under the wing of my guardian angel in a meditation, I asked the Holy Spirit to show me what demon—what fear—it was that was rising to the surface of my consciousness. Not all were easy to vanquish. Some took a few seconds, others took days. Some came in pairs, others in groups of ten, others alone. Most amazing to me was how attached I'd become to them. Like the routine of daily life, I knew them. They were mine. And despite the drain on my energy, I was accustomed to life with them. Strangely, I found myself occasionally more afraid of living without the fear, than I was of the fear itself.

The one constant was the way the fear was presented to me. Just as in my first meditation and discovery, a memory from my past would pop into my head. Most were long forgotten and I had to struggle to understand their significance. I quickly learned, however, that the memory was raised because it signified a fear or limiting belief that I had to confront.

At the end of the two weeks, I was facing a handful of memories. They had hit me like a staccato burst of machine gun fire. I struggled with them for three days. Despite nightly meditations, visits to church and counsel from Elisabeth, I wasn't making any further progress in deciphering their meaning.

Presently, Angélique returned with the book and crayons.

"What do you want to color?" I asked.

"Not color—draw," she corrected me.

"Okay. What do you want to draw?"

She set her chin on her hand and played with her long blond hair. "A flower."

"Go ahead."

"No, daddy. I want *you* to draw it."

"I have an idea. I'll draw it, and, you color it in."

She nodded her approval.

We began our project. Without asking permission, she hoisted herself onto my lap, all the while watching my black pencil create a flower where there had been nothing.

"I love you," I told her.

She smiled and lifted her shoulders. I wanted her to be a strong woman—confident and bold. She was well on her way. But, it was still precious to see the shy little girl in her make an appearance now and then.

"I chose you."

I didn't think I had heard her correctly. "Excuse me?"

She turned to look me in the eye. "I chose you—you and Maman."

I smiled a goofy smile—a sure sign a parent is clueless. "Chose us for what?"

"To be my parents," she said with a large dose of exasperation.

I leaned back in my chair, shook my head, and squinted. My body was going through the motions of bewilderment, but, inside me, I understood exactly what she meant. "Before you were born?"

"*Oui*. I chose you and *Maman* to be my parents."

"Why?" Now, I was the child.

She sighed, turning back to the drawing. "Sometimes, I wonder."

I sat there motionless, staring at my little girl. After what had transpired over the previous two weeks, I didn't think anything could stun me. Obviously, I was wrong. It seemed that every time I became complacent or too pleased with myself, my angel either brewed up a storm inside me or sent one of my children to remind me just how far behind the learning curve I was.

I was not ready to contemplate my daughter's words. I knew there was a reason for her timing. I knew that I would have to fully consider what she said at some point. But, as I've already described, so much of what was happening and so much of what had happened, were seeds planted inside of me that would bloom on an unknown date under unknown circumstances.

Elisabeth and Christophe arrived. I was still in a stupor, my mind completely shut off. How do you *think* about your child's announcement that she chose you to be her father? I shared what had happened with them.

Unlike me, Camille, Elisabeth and Christophe, while marveling at Angélique, were not knocked off their mental feet.

Several hours later, after the children had been tucked in, the four of us remained on the balcony. It had been a pleasant evening. Christophe remained as quiet as ever, although he had interjected a comment or observation on occasion. Elisabeth turned to Camille. My sister's eyes sparkled, a sure sign she had been waiting to delve into the topic she was now ready to lay before us.

"What do you think about all of this?"

"You mean, what Eric has been going through?"

Elisabeth nodded.

"I think it's fantastic. He's been a different person lately." There was a reservation in her voice and we all heard it.

"But what?" I asked.

"Well, I can't say that I understand all of it. I have to admit, too, that it scares me a little. Especially, after you told me about the demons." She shuddered.

"What don't you understand?" I asked.

"Most of it, actually. These memories you have. And the feelings you have. What does it all mean?"

"Ever since we've been married, you've complained about me not being loving enough with the children, or, that I don't take risks, or, I'm not spontaneous. And, lately, you've noticed how bitter I've become."

"All true."

Everybody laughed. "You don't have to agree with everything," I said.

"I'll stop you when you're wrong," Camille responded with that naughty smile of hers. "What do your past experiences have to do with your behavior today?"

"They have programmed me to act a certain way. I have to remember what happened in order to reprogram myself."

My wife was frowning. I didn't see Elisabeth or Christophe asserting agreement, either.

"That's not true," Camille said after several seconds of reflection. "You're not an automaton."

"I know, but certain things that happened when I was younger were having an effect on me as an adult."

Camille nodded. "Sure, but only because you let them. But, don't say you were programmed, like you had no choice."

"She's right," Elisabeth chimed in. "You're not a slave to those past events or emotions. The fact that you dealt with them and overcame them proves it."

I took a deep breath and scratched my head. "Yeah, you're right. The idea of being programmed is wrong. Let's just say that I made certain choices as a child, like giving up my power in the one case to my father and grandfather. Now, I'm making new choices." It was making more sense to me. "That's exactly what it is. It's a new choice."

"*That* I can understand," said Camille.

"How about you?" Elisabeth asked.

"What about me?" said Camille.

"Have you had any of these experiences?"

Camille's head bobbed back and forth as she tried to script an answer. "I haven't had the same *intense* experiences like Eric. But, there have been many things from my childhood that I've come to terms with."

"Such as?"

"Well, Eric has criticized my parents a lot in the past and—"

"Wait a minute," I interrupted. "Let's not get into that."

"Why not?" said Camille. "It's important."

I cringed. If ever there was a hot button that I could push to launch my wife into the ionosphere of defensiveness and anger, it was criticism of her parents. She took it so personally. I used to admire the way she'd defend them. But it soon became tiresome and I realized that her defense of them was blind. There was no rhyme or reason to her behavior that I could sense. In her eyes, they had to be defended even if the critique was patently accurate.

This was not an issue I wanted to visit at the moment. But, Camille would not be dissuaded.

"I don't have to defend everything my parents did anymore." She laughed as I nearly fell off my chair. "I'm serious. I've realized that I'm different and that I do things differently. I used to think that meant condemning them. And when you'd criticize them, it made me feel guilty for doing things differently. But, now, I realize that's not true. We all do what we can when we can."

"You really mean that?"

"I love my parents," she continued. "They did the best they could and did what they thought was good for us. For some reason, I believed that if I didn't follow their example, it would be unfaithful, or ... I don't know. It just seemed wrong."

"That's what I don't understand about you, Camille." I took her hand. "Most people—myself included—repeat the mistakes of our parents, all the while, swearing we'll do just the opposite. You, defending your parents to the death, have always taken any negatives from your youth and turned them into positives for our children. You've always had the strangest way of defending their mistakes while following only their good examples. It's an amazing trait."

"Like what?" asked Elisabeth. "Can you give me an example?"

Camille was silent, so, I volunteered to fill her in. "For example, when Camille was a child, she was often dropped off at church on Sunday mornings. Her parents didn't go because they were running a restaurant. Often, they forgot to pick her up. Other times, they were thirty or forty minutes late picking her up from school. The school and church were just two miles from the house, but the only road was a busy one and frequented by gypsies."

"I can't tell you how many times strange men stopped their cars and asked me to get in," Camille said, hugging herself.

"Another thing that bothered her was that she had to awaken her parents to take her to school. That meant that she ate breakfast alone and was responsible, at a pretty young age, to make sure that not only she, but her parents as well, got up early enough to get to school on time.

"But, she's just the opposite with our children. She's up, showered and dressed before any of them. She makes them breakfast. They're never late for school. She's always waiting when they get out."

Camille shrugged. "I want what's best for my children."

"How did you deal with those feelings from your childhood?" asked Elisabeth. "I'd like to know, because I've had trouble facing certain things."

"Who says I have?" asked Camille.

Elizabeth frowned. "I don't understand. How can you treat your children completely differently if you haven't overcome those feelings?"

"I don't know."

"She's amazing," I said.

"I'd like to get rid of the feelings," Camille continued. "I'd like to do what Eric has done. But, I'm afraid. Eric had to experience the same emotions all over again. I don't know if I can do that."

"Why are you afraid?" asked Elisabeth.

"Because I don't like those feelings. I don't want to bring them back."

"But that's the point," I said. "We can ignore them, but that doesn't mean they've gone anywhere."

"I'm afraid."

"Afraid of what? What's worse—experiencing the feelings or living your whole life with them?"

Camille swallowed. I could see the resolve in her face. I prayed silently that she'd be able to do it. It was so obvious that she wanted to. Suddenly, her eyes took on a far-off glaze. She closed them momentarily and wrapped her arms around herself. "I was scared. I was just a little girl. I felt like they didn't love me." Her eyes started to water.

"Get rid of those feelings," I said.

"How?"

"The fright and the lack of love—do you feel them somewhere in your body?"

"Here," Camille said, pointing to her stomach.

"Grab it and throw it away. Throw the negative emotions back to your parents."

"I can't do that. They weren't trying to hurt me."

"You've got to get pissed."

Camille looked sadly at me. "But, I love my parents."

"This isn't about hating them," I said. "It's about making a new choice. You have to choose not to harbor those feelings anymore. You've held onto them since childhood. It's time to get rid of them. They serve no purpose. Give them back to your parents."

"Wait a second," Elisabeth interrupted. "If Camille doesn't feel it's right to throw the negative feelings she has at anyone, then, she shouldn't."

"What should I do with them?"

"How about recycling them?" Elisabeth suggested. "Just like we use compost to nourish the soil and help plants grow, try offering the negative energy from your emotions to the earth, to be recycled as something positive."

What I saw next amazed me. Camille had no need of meditation. She needed no further explanation or prompting. She had access to her emotions like I had access to the coins in my pocket.

Her face reddened. Her eyes overflowed. Her brow wrinkled. She reached to her stomach, grabbed and threw the invisible feelings down to the ground.

"I don't want it anymore," she said with anguish. "I'm fed up!" Her voice was becoming more assertive. "Take it!" she yelled. "I didn't deserve that!" With each statement, she threw more away. "Take it!" Shaking her head, she yelled again, "Take it! I don't want it anymore!" She cried freely, still throwing more feelings to the earth. Through her tears, her eyes stared straight ahead, oblivious to the three of us sitting around the table.

We watched her for five minutes. Sometimes, she sobbed. Sometimes, she was silent. Sometimes, she yelled. Through it all, she continued emptying herself of whatever it was that she had been carrying.

Finally, Camille laughed through her tears. "I need a tissue."

I jumped up and ran to the bathroom. I felt an unexpected swell of emotion inside me. What she had just done took an incredible amount of courage. It also took an incredible amount of strength. How could she have such access to those emotions?

I handed her the tissue and kissed her forehead.

"How do you feel now?" I asked.

"Lighter than air," Camille responded with an effervescent smile.

"And you didn't even need to meditate," I noted in wonder.

She turned to me. "That was something else I wanted to ask you. Why do you need to meditate?"

"I just need to. Things become clearer to me when I meditate. It's the only way for my guardian angel to talk to me."

"I hear my guardian angel all the time."

I shifted uncomfortably in my chair. Wincing, I asked, "*Ta petite voix?*"

Her nod tightened the knot in my stomach.

"Her little voice?" asked Elisabeth.

Camille looked at me with raised eyebrows. I was going to have to confess publicly.

"Since before we were married, Camille often told me she thought she was going crazy because she could hear a voice talking to her. She knew it wasn't just her imagination because the voice was always right and told her things she couldn't possibly know. For example, she told me before Angélique was born, and before we knew what gender she was, that her voice told her that our first four children would be a girl, then three boys."

"I remember you saying that," Elisabeth said in amazement.

"Well, I made fun of her. I told her that she *was* going crazy because only lunatics heard voices. I called it '*her little voice.*' She stopped telling me about what the voice told her. But," I said, looking at my wife, "I doubt that it stopped."

"No, of course, it didn't stop. I eventually realized it was my angel giving me messages."

"And one of the messages was that we should not invest in a certain business venture that I was offered a piece of. I dismissed Camille and her little voice out of hand. I lost a hundred percent of our investment."

"That's so cool," Christophe said. "Not losing the money, I mean—that you hear a voice so clearly."

"I'm sorry, Camille," I said.

"Now, do you believe in my voice?" she asked.

"Absolutely. In fact, I always have. But, if I gave too much credence to it, I'd have to admit something lacking in me. In other words, how come I didn't get such clear guidance?"

"Have you been able to figure out the rest of your memories?" Elisabeth asked me.

"No. And I don't want to talk about it right now."

"Why not?" said Camille.

"Let's keep talking about you."

"What's wrong?"

"Nothing. I just haven't made any headway and there's no point in pushing it. Besides, I think what Camille did tonight was fantastic and ..."

"What?"

I had to swallow. I didn't know why, but my chest felt heavy and I was moved. I tried to close my eyes, hoping it would subside. It was about as controllable as a rising tide. I began to shake. "I love you, Camille. I love you so much." The tide kept rising, overflowing through my eyes. "You're incredible. You're amazing. What are you doing with me?"

Camille's eyes were still red from a few minutes earlier. Tears flowed anew. "That's a silly question. Because I love you."

"But I don't deserve you. I don't deserve your love." There was no holding back. I was sobbing.

Elisabeth and Christophe looked on, but it didn't matter. What I felt—an incredible love for my wife and the sensation that I didn't deserve her love—had complete control over me.

Camille waved me over.

I moved quickly around the table and buried my face in her chest, my body shaking. "I love you."

"I love you, too," she answered, stroking my hair.

I pulled a chair next to her. "But, why?"

She smiled. "Because of who you are."

I shook my head in confusion. "I don't get it." I looked to Elisabeth for an answer. She, too, was crying.

"You guys are awesome," she said.

"But, why do you love me?"

Wiping a tear from my face, she said, "That's what the problem is, isn't it?"

"What problem?"

"You got a lot of answers from your meditations," asked Camille, "and from going back to certain events in your childhood, right?"

I nodded.

"But," Camille continued, "the last few memories and meditations didn't yield an answer."

"So?"

"You had to experience this catharsis," Elisabeth explained.

But I still did not understand.

"You believe," my wife stated sadly, "that you don't deserve to be loved."

She may as well have stabbed me through the heart. The truth knocked me back onto my chair. Once the effect of the blow subsided, my question remained. "But why do you love me?"

"Do you love yourself?"

"That's not the point."

"That's everything," Elisabeth said. "It doesn't matter whether someone else loves you if you don't love yourself."

"And," Camille said, "you can't really love someone else if you can't love yourself."

The conversation continued, but I remained unconvinced—more accurately, unmoved. My feelings for Camille showed me the problem. But the words offered by my sister, Christophe and my wife did not solve it.

After Camille and I had gone to bed, I was still grappling with the matter. I realized that I had to believe that I was lovable—I had to love myself. But, I didn't know how to make me love myself.

I was too tired for a meditation. Besides, I had spent the last three days meditating and it hadn't gotten me any closer to even figuring out what the problem was.

So, I prayed.

"Guardian angel, I love you. God, I love you. I trust, but help my mistrust. You always said that you'd never give us a burden that we couldn't carry. I need to figure this out. Meet me halfway. Actually, I don't know if I'm even one percent of the way. Wherever I am, meet me."

I expected an immediate answer. Not just expected, I knew I'd get an answer. I knew it in my gut. And, I did.

It wasn't a bolt of lightning. It wasn't even a tickle on my cheek from my guardian angel's feathers. It was a simple thought: "If I love you, who are you to say you're not deserving of love?"

◐   ◐   ◐

My spiritual journey continued over the next three months at a fevered pitch. Although I did not have to go through the constant hell of feeling, then deciphering, then ridding new limiting beliefs and fears on a daily basis, there was always something occurring inside of me. I had completed what seemed like my fiftieth edit of *The Soul Collectors* in October. I knew that yet another edit was required. It was a work of my mind and not of my heart. By January, the final edit was complete. Also at that time, I had begun working with energy. With each old fear or limiting belief that I discarded, I had more energy to direct in a positive direction.

It was my passion for writing that had plunged me into this dangerous spiritual current. When Elisabeth asked me why I hadn't yet been published, though I tried to fight it, I knew nobody was to blame except myself. Moreover, I knew my writing would never be what it could be as long as my heart was closed off to the world.

I decided it was time to use my energy to make the leap from aspiring writer to full-time author. Through a friend, I had gotten my manuscript into the hands of one of the premier literary agencies in Paris. Two weeks had gone by and there was no news. Normally, it took as much as six weeks before judgment was passed on a manuscript. I didn't care. I was going to use my energy to effect a specific result on a specific day. It was Monday. I decided that I would hear from the agent on Thursday and that she would beg me to sign on with their agency. I, along with Elisabeth, my mother and Camille sent positive energy to that agent Monday, Tuesday and Wednesday.

Thursday morning arrived. I was confident. I was sure. This was going to happen. I continued to send positive energy to the nameless, faceless agent in Paris. "You love my book. You want my book. You can't wait to call me and sign me up." This was the message I sent her over and over again.

Camille, my mother and Elisabeth called me every thirty minutes. And each time, I had nothing to report other than waning confidence.

My confidence peaked at noon. From noon to four, it was a free-fall. I watched each minute pass. By five, I was ready to leave the office, go straight to a bar and drown my disappointment. But, I still held out hope. Finally, at a quarter to seven, Camille convinced me to come home.

Two weeks later, I received a fax. It was a blistering attack on my book and the conclusion—wholly unnecessary—stated that the agency did not wish to represent me.

The fallout from that debacle varied.

Elisabeth took the defeat very personally. She was livid with God for not fulfilling His side of the bargain.

My mother was also irritated, but it was much less intense. She decided that it meant the book should be self-published.

Camille was upset for me. She also realized that she was no longer going to wait for *Godot.*

My spiritual journey was suddenly in a circling pattern. That which mattered most to me wasn't served by these new insights. There were, however, two saving graces. I knew I was a better person because of the spiritual work I had done. I also knew that *The Soul Collectors* was—although not published—better because of the changes in me. So, while meditations stopped and energy work came to a complete halt, the foundation remained.

Instead of meditating, I read voraciously. Most of the books on spirituality were either manuals on elevating man to the status of gods, or, they were guides leading to a destination I did not deem the goal of the quest. Others were helpful in explaining what was happening. My mind had not completely given up the reins. In fact, it demanded to catch up with the rest of me. So, I assertively sought out information that offered explanations on how spirituality worked. The information was necessarily conveyed via symbolism. Nevertheless, my mind was assuaged; sometimes, even excited. What surprised me most was that so many of the authors, or, in the case of cassettes, the speakers, had incredible insights, but, for some reason—prejudice or some other myopia—they failed to make the last step in the logical chain of the syllogism. They seemed to lose sight of the big picture at the very last minute.

These investigations raised questions in my own mind and heart. Why, over so many years of studying philosophy and religion, matters which dealt with the nonphysical realm, did I fail to make the last step? And, what was it that finally pushed me over the proverbial top?

Looking back, I could see the desire to know and to feel more. I was forever in a quest to understand the higher order of life. But, I obviously held back. I pursued knowledge, not feeling. And my body reacted. For years, it had been screaming at me.

Since age seven or eight, I had been extremely vulnerable to illness. I was allergic to just about every living organism on land or in the sea. I had the dubious distinction of contracting mononucleosis twice, when one bout immunized everyone else. I had had pneumonia, scarlet fever, more than one hundred cases of strep-throat. I was such a good case study that my pediatrician wrote an article about me. I missed more than three months of school when I was sixteen. At least one time each year, one of my myriad fevers rose to the point of delirium. On one occasion, I was spending the night with my grandparents. I went to sleep, weakened by the fever. I awakened with my grandfather holding me down while my grandmother tried to stop my nose from bleeding. It seems that I thought the house was on fire and tried to jump from their second-story window. My grandfather reached through the window and caught me just in time. On another occasion, while my family was vacationing in the mountains, I ran screaming through the hotel at three in the morning. I thought an avalanche was crushing the hotel.

Two months after Camille and I were married, another ailment was added to my bag of tricks—migraines. I had been prone to headaches my entire life. When a particularly bad one developed, I sometimes described it as a migraine. I learned the hard way the vast difference in degree between a bad headache and a migraine.

I went to bed early on a Saturday night, suffering from a "bad" headache that was rapidly escalating in intensity. I knew it was different than all of my previous headaches. Thirty minutes later, Camille was in our room crying, unsure of what to do, scared I was going to die. I was on all fours in our bed, slamming my head against the wall. There was no thought process involved other than to strike at the pain, whatever the cost. Somehow, she got me into the car and to the hospital. The doctors sedated me and performed a cat-scan. It showed nothing, of course. In the ensuing five years, the migraines arrived with greater frequency—eventually establishing a pattern: one every two weeks. I saw every neurologist within four hundred kilometers of Lyon. They prescribed barbiturates, caffeine pills and self-administered injections of a new anti-migraine drug out of England. The doctors agreed on two things—my migraines were one of the severest forms, and, I would *hopefully* outgrow them in fifteen to twenty years. There was no cause other than genetics, they said. My only resort was to stanch the effects.

Had I been working for anyone else other than my boss, Pascal DeLorier, I would have been fired inside of my first year of work. I missed work at least once a month, sometimes for an entire week, due to illness or migraines. He never complained. On the contrary, anytime he saw me pale and shivering from the effects of a fever, he sent me home. He never questioned my veracity, either; which was amazing given the fact that it was rare for a man in his twenties to suffer from migraines and rarer still for any adult to be so sick as often as I was. He was not really a boss. He was a mentor, a friend, a surrogate father, and an angel of sorts.

It was not until three months after my journey began that I realized I had not been sick or suffered a migraine in a long time—three months, to be exact. It was my boss who noticed first and asked me. I was as surprised as he was. Later that day, I understood the meaning of the timing.

It has now been almost a year since I began practicing spirituality, not just religion. I have been ill just once. I have suffered no more migraines. I don't pretend to understand the how's and why's of my illnesses and migraines, let alone how and why they stopped when they did. I've read myriad analyses and theories that are all beyond my comprehension. I do know, however, that the body and soul are not two strangers living together. They work in concert. They're married. When the soul is suffering, the body signals as much. I don't know whether all diseases and ailments are purely physical manifestations of metaphysical conditions. But, my pains and illnesses have been either warnings or challenges to make a change; whether the change be growth, a new direction or a strengthening of the will.

Free of illness and migraines, I would have thought that I'd have a new perspective on work—a more positive outlook. I did have a new perspective, but it was not positive. I was growing more restless. My home life was improving, growing and changing at a rapid pace. Personally, I was improving. But my writing was dead in the water. What was my professional future? I wondered. The atmosphere at my office wasn't to blame. I loved my boss and his brother; I enjoyed my co-workers. It was not the job nor the people surrounding me that were inadequate. Everything else was changing and my work had to change, too.

When winter hit Lyon, our youngest, Cédric, who was born the previous April, proved incapable of enduring the cold. Like Camille, he suffered from weeping eczema. In the cold, dry climate, his skin dried up in blotches, then erupted. The sores remained open for days or weeks at a time and oozed like a bad burn. Thus, the term *weeping* eczema. Three times during the winter, his open sores were infected by a dangerous strain of strep. He was allergic to penicillin. As a result, there was no way to quickly and effectively treat him. Camille had long since eschewed antibiotics, but resorted to them in dangerous cases such as strep because the homeopathic remedies were not sufficient. According to the pediatricians and dermatologists, there were only two ways to eliminate his condition—give him weekly doses of cortisone, a steroid, or move to a tropical or subtropical climate. Pumping a steroid into our nine-month old was out of the question.

Whether we would have contemplated moving, assuming Cédric did not suffer from the cold, is a question that is difficult to answer. For years, Camille and I talked about leaving Lyon and moving to a warmer climate, away from the big city. But that dream was contingent upon my selling a book. And not just any book contract. I'd done the math. I had figured out exactly how much of an advance we needed in order to quit my job in Lyon and move elsewhere, dependent only upon my royalties and future book contracts. But, the contingency existed only in my head, not Camille's.

After I failed in February to force the agent in Paris to sign me up, Camille began her campaign anew, bothering me about moving. She had many good reasons, as she always had. The children could not play outside without coats, gloves and boots for several months. Lyon was not an idyllic setting. We both missed the sea, she having grown up by the sea and I having spent several months each year at the seashore. But those reasons had always been outweighed by Reality. Reality was represented by a balance sheet. On one side was my salary, on the other was the cost of living and raising four children. Reality was simply an overwhelming argument.

Don't get me wrong. I never won the argument. Camille never agreed that the scales were tipped by Reality. But, I had veto power. When choosing between inaction and action, the spouse opting for inaction always has veto power.

But Cédric's condition tipped the scales. And it changed Reality. What's the exchange rate for the health of a child? I couldn't come up with an equivalent in French francs. I didn't even try.

Without a doubt, it was the deciding factor. But with everything that had happened in the previous months, I would like to believe that my son did not have to suffer in order for me to make that decision. In truth, I think that my angel, in cahoots with Cédric's angel, decided to give me a boost. And, if the two angels decided to give me a boost, I must have needed it.

It was a Saturday in March. Elisabeth and Christophe were again at our house. They were recently engaged to be married and we were celebrating. It seemed that they were present for all of our momentous events—not as bystanders but as catalysts. We were discussing our dreams, hopes, plans for the next two, five and ten years. Christophe was getting more and more involved in the conversations. I assumed, therefore, that the conversations were becoming more nonlinear.

"Why haven't any of your books been published?" Elisabeth asked me.

"That's one of many questions I haven't been able to answer," I admitted. "It has yet to be the right time."

"What do you mean by the right time?" asked Camille.

"There are two possibilities that I can envision. God knows what's best, and, it's not yet best for me to be a full-time author. Or, I'm unconsciously limiting myself, sabotaging myself in some way. I'm not really worried about it for the moment, though."

"I'm worried," Camille said. "As long as you're going to wait to get published before we can move, I'm *very* worried."

"Maybe that's the problem," Christophe said. "You're waiting for a book contract instead of just *doing* something on your own."

"Don't you think I'll ever get published?" I asked him.

"I'm sure you will. But, it will happen when you're not looking for it—not *waiting* for it."

"Well?" Camille said.

"What?"

"Why don't we stop waiting and start doing?"

I looked around the table. Elisabeth, Christophe and Camille all had a look in their eyes. Like parents waiting for their child to take the first step. They knew what was at hand. I sensed something, but I didn't realize what. That ignorance allowed me to make the step.

"What the hell," I said. "Why not?"

"You're serious?" asked Camille.

"I am."

"You won't change your mind in a couple of hours, or, tomorrow, or, next week?"

I put my hand on my heart. "I give you my word. We're going." It was a frightening promise, but it felt right.

"That's fantastic." Elisabeth was beaming.

"Where?" asked Christophe.

I was caught up in the energy of the moment. I felt free and wild. "Let's go to Australia." Camille and I had dreamt of visiting Australia. It was too far to go for less than two weeks. Besides, it was a very expensive trip. If I could get a job there, our vacation could be replaced by a permanent move.

"That's perfect," Camille agreed.

We cut short the conversation. Camille and I had to attend a function sponsored by one of my clients. Elisabeth and Christophe stayed to take care of the children. On our way to the restaurant, we were still discussing our newly decided-upon move.

"Australia is pretty far," Camille observed.

"True."

"And it would be expensive to fly back every year to see our families."

I laughed. "Way too expensive. We'd have to count on them coming to see us."

She turned to look out the window.

"Are you having second thoughts?" I asked.

"Not about moving. Just about Australia."

"Yeah, I agree. We should pick someplace closer to home."

By the time we arrived home from our dinner, we had settled on l'Ile de Ré, a small island off France's Atlantic coast. Elisabeth and Christophe were surprised by the quick change in destination, but were happy that we were going to take action, regardless of where it led us.

◈　　　◈　　　◈

Over the course of the next week, I studied the small island. I discovered that its real estate was some of the most expensive in the country, outside of Paris. Moreover, there was not much demand for professionals. The island's economy was based on agriculture and tourism. Once again, I resorted to a balance sheet. The move did not make sense on paper. So, Camille and I considered other options—more realistic options. As long as we were going somewhere warm, Cédric would be healthy and Camille would approve.

We settled on the Riviera. While tourism was certainly a staple on the Côte d'Azur, there were numerous large cities where I could find work. It did not matter which city as long as it was not Marseilles. Marseilles was a large, cosmopolitan city on the Mediterranean, but it suffered from one of the worst crime rates in France.

You may find this series of decisions—or, more accurately, indecisions—crazy, laughable, even irresponsible given the fact that we were dragging four children with us. You would not be alone. Many in my family thought we had lost our minds. Not about moving per se. Simply because we never settled on one place for more than a few hours, a few days at most. But we were committed to making a change. And the Riviera seemed the safest, best bet.

Two days later, after waiting to see if we would change our destination again, I told my boss that we were leaving. He was naturally shocked, but understood that family came first. He offered to assist me in finding work on the Riviera. If I changed my mind about leaving in the interim, I knew that I might look foolish, but I also knew that I would still have a job. So, it wasn't an irreversible step. Nevertheless, it was a crucial one. Telling someone outside my family—and Pascal was the most important person to me outside my clan—committed me.

While I rested on the accomplishment of telling Pascal, Camille went into high gear. She organized a garage sale, arranged to put our condo on the market, contacted schools in Nice, Cannes, and several other cities along the coast. All the while, she pushed me to draft my curriculum vitae and to send out letters to prospective firms.

Pascal contacted an attorney he knew in Marseilles. I was adamant about not living in Marseilles, but the firm had offices all along the Riviera. After just one phone call, the attorney invited me down for a get-together. I thought that meant an interview. The real purpose was to sell me on Marseilles.

Before I knew it, I had an offer to work in Marseilles. Granted it was not our first choice of locale. But it was a terrific job offer. The work was the same, meaning I needed no new training. It was a perfect fit. Camille and I could hardly believe it. Everything had fallen into place so quickly. It was all the proof we needed that we were making the right choice.

There was only one problem. We couldn't leave until we sold our condo. We certainly couldn't afford to own two homes. So, I told my future employer that I would be moving down to Marseilles just as soon as we had our house under contract.

We could relax. The sale of the condo was beyond our control. Everything else was in place. We were set.

All we had to do was wait. For the first time in a long time, we knew where we were going and what we were going to do. It's exactly at those times—when you're warm and comfortable—that your angel pulls off the covers and throws open the windows. "Time to wake up!"

On July 1, Camille and I left with our children for a small village in the French alps where my parents had taken up residence shortly before the death of my dad. It was the site of Elisabeth's and Christophe's wedding.

With all of our planning for the move, the short search for work, and then follow-up research of schools and neighborhoods in Marseilles, we had almost forgotten about the impending nuptials.

The wedding was small by modern standards—only seventy guests and family members. Since all guests ex-

cept our family were staying in hotels, and since everyone except my mother and younger brother needed an
entire day of traveling to get to the wedding, it was a
four-day event. We arrived on Tuesday, the last of the
Pétris clan to settle in.

In my younger days, I loved Alpe-d'Huez. Nestled
in the French alps, the mountain village was difficult to
access. A dangerously winding road climbed into the sky,
finally spilling into the hamlet at the base of a large peak.
Many of the buildings on the main street were the origi-
nal wood structures reminiscent of another era. Unlike
the larger, more developed ski resorts like Chamonix
and Flan, Alpe-d'Huez guarded its rustic alpine charm.

Since I had been married, however, I disliked the
town. Actually, it was not the town, itself, I disliked. I
had lost interest in skiing and, therefore, was bored there
in the winter. The last time we had visited was at Christ-
mas with all four children. The children were suffering
from chicken pox and every room in the house was over-
occupied. All six of us stayed in the same room for six
days. I swore I would not return. Elisabeth and
Christophe proved me wrong when they announced their
plans to marry there.

As we drove up the precipitous mountain road, ver-
dant valleys, oceans of pine trees, and royal peaks crowned
by snow, stretched in every direction. At each turn, a

vista more magnificent than the last appeared magically. I had forgotten how beautiful the Alps were in the summer. As the air grew lighter, so did our moods. With no grand expectations and our minds more concerned about the impending move to Marseilles, the majesty of the mountains caught us by surprise.

We arrived at my mother's house, its immense windows framing mountains and blue sky. We sensed something special. By the evening of that first day, I realized what a spiritually rich place it was. Far from the city, the dirt, and the crime, with clean air and mountain springs, populated more by vegetation and wildlife than people, Alpe-d'Huez was more a spiritual retreat than a resort town.

We had left Lyon under steamy humidity and a gray sky. We arrived against brisk breezes and under a powder blue sky. Our bodies instantly released the emergency brakes and coasted.

My siblings recognized my attitude within minutes of our arrival. I was flying. I felt wonderful. Something fantastic was at hand and I threw my chips into the pot.

The first night was a dinner at my mother's house. It was my first opportunity to meet Christophe's parents. The Pétris family is about as easy to infiltrate as Saint Cyre, France's most prestigious school. But his parents made themselves at home and jumped into the celebration with both feet. Shortly after their arrival, a priest walked onto the patio where we were eating dinner. Père Brion was going to preside at the wedding mass. He was more than their family priest, however. He had taught Christophe's father and, then, Christophe and his two brothers.

Père Brion sat next to me and the sparks began to fill the night sky. My brothers and sisters looked on in horror, while Christophe's family was too shocked to react. He and I teased each other mercilessly. He was a Jesuit and I accused his Order of trying to destroy the Catholic Church and overthrow the Pope in the process. He called me a heretic. I told him that I should probably write his sermon for him. He told me I was going to hell. Unbeknownst to the two families gathered around us, we were hitting it off beautifully.

After the teasing subsided, we smiled at each other, and I began asking him questions. How did he maintain his passion after more than fifty years in the priesthood? What did he do to grow spiritually? How did he view my generation?

He smiled at me, a twinkle in his blue eyes. "Wait until Saturday," he said. "You'll have the answers you need on Saturday."

I couldn't wait to hear his sermon. It was strange, however. A sermon didn't allow a discussion. It was, by definition, a monologue.

Later that night, with the children in bed, I sat out on the patio, staring up at the sky. There was no moon. It looked like a jeweler's black velvet display with thousands of diamonds of varying sizes spread sporadically for the choosing. I hadn't looked much to the sky in Lyon. In any case, it was difficult to see many stars due to the city lights. My soul seemed to expand with the change in perspective. I reminded myself to stop looking down all the time. Look beyond the five meters around you, I told myself. See the opportunities that abound. They're all within sight. If only we would look.

Camille opened the door to the patio. "Phone call, Eric. It's Pascal."

I laughed. Someone was playing a practical joke on me. There was no reason for my boss to call me. "Sure." I laid back down.

"I'm serious," she insisted. Her voice convinced me.

I jogged into the kitchen and picked up the phone. "*Âllo?*"

"Eric, it's Pascal," my boss's voice sounded through the receiver. "I hate to bother you, but we've got a problem."

"What's wrong?"

"The pleadings in the Rousellière case that you did. We sent the originals to the client for execution and they never arrived. We tried to get into your computer, but couldn't. Can you talk me through it?"

I smiled to myself. That was the price I had to pay for suggesting that we computerize the firm. I was the only person in the firm with any computing experience. As a result, my job description was both *maître* and computer repairman.

"Go ahead."

"Okay. The computer is on. What do I do?"

"You're in Windows, right?"

"How can I tell?"

"There should be a bunch of icons on the screen, a toolbar at the top—"

"I see them. Alright."

"One of the icons looks like a file. It's got the firm name on it."

"Got it."

"Double click on that file."

"Okay, I'm double-clicking. Now, I've got a whole list of things."

"Those are more files. There's a file for each client. They're in alphabetical order, so look for Rousellière."

"I don't see it. There's Rambaud, then, the next is Santoine."

"Damn." I gave him a dozen other directions, including a file search, but none led to the Rousellière file.

"Don't we have copies?"

"No. I checked. The problem is that the pleadings have to be filed in court tomorrow."

I scratched my head. "I know that file is on my computer."

"Don't worry. I'll keep trying."

"I'll come in tomorrow morning."

"Don't be silly," Pascal said. "You're not going to miss your sister's wedding."

"I'll leave early tomorrow, spend no more than an hour in the office; I'll be back here tomorrow night. Besides, tomorrow is Wednesday and the wedding is not until Saturday."

"I'm sorry about this."

That was just like him. It was, in every respect, *his* firm. But, he never treated me as an employee. "Don't be sorry. If you can't find the file on the computer, it's my fault. I'll see you around ten-thirty tomorrow morning."

Nobody in the house was happy about my sudden turnaround, least of all myself. I had my heart set on river-rafting. I had taken up crew in Lyon and we had booked two canoes in addition to the larger, guided rafts—one canoe for Christophe and one for me. But, family came first. That was Pascal's motto. And, over the past several years, he had become part of my family. As a result, it was not work that was calling me back, it was loyalty to a family member. And, besides, I was only going to miss one day's worth of festivities, even if the river-rafting was what I most wanted to do. In twenty-four hours, I would be back on the patio, under the stars, with a gin and tonic in my hand.

❈   ❈   ❈

Cars were at a premium on Wednesday. Half the crew was heading fifty kilometers from Alpe-d'Huez for a day of river rafting. My three boys were going fishing with their uncles and cousins. Camille was planning to help my sisters pick up new arrivals from the train station in Bourg-d'Oisans, just down the valley from Alpe-d'Huez. I would take the train, I decided. I was in need of some rest and could not imagine making that drive three times in thirty-six hours. Besides, there were no cars available with all the activities on the agenda.

I arrived in Lyon by ten, thanks in large part to the TGV connection at Grenoble. I spent no more than fifteen minutes in the office. I was livid—with nobody to blame except myself.

There was no question in my mind the night before that I'd saved the documents. Rousellière was a new file, not in the office, but on my computer. I had only been working the case for four days. The pleadings were voluminous and I had used documents from a closed file as a template. Since hard disk space was at a premium, I routinely copied all closed files from my computer onto floppy disks. I had inadvertently copied the Rousellière pleadings onto the same floppy disk.

My task at the office completed, I looked forward to surprising Camille with an early return. I happened upon a skilled taxi driver who weaved his way to the train station just in time for me to catch the TGV back to Grenoble.

There are times when I am terribly ashamed of France. The paralyzing strikes, our Chamberlin-esque "peace at all costs" foreign policy, confiscatory taxes, and socialist government come immediately to mind. But, there are other times, when my blood runs the blue, white and red of the Tri-Color and I hum the *Marseillaise*. Sitting in a first class compartment on a TGV as it pulls out of the station, then, accelerating to 200 k.p.h., was one of those times. It was an engineering miracle. As with all things French, at least as important as its ability to function properly was its sleek and handsome appearance.

I always treated myself to a first class ticket when traveling on the TGV. It wasn't that much more expensive than second class, and the company was cleaner and quieter, the compartments less crowded. When I arrived at the *guichet*, however, the attendant informed me that all first class seats were sold.

"That's ridiculous," I responded. "Check again. I'm not traveling second class."

"I assure you, *monsieur*, first class is completely booked. There is space in first class, however, on your connection from Grenoble to Alpe-d'Huez."

"Well, just give me a first class ticket for both trains and I'm sure I'll find a vacancy on the TGV. First class is never fully occupied."

"Sorry, sir, but I can't give you a seat since all are reserved—whether everybody with a reservation boards or not."

This was ridiculous. Yet another example of our government's colossal stupidity in an attempt to fill its coffers. Like airplanes, all first class TGV trains had assigned seats. And, each seat required a reservation. The reservation could be made at the train station a minute before departure or months in advance. Unlike airlines, however, the SNCF charged a fee for reservations. I had set my heart on traveling in first and I was not going to be disappointed by the functionary sitting behind the metal bars. "Let me see the manager."

"There's nothing she can do about it. As I've already told you, first class is booked. Now, do you want a second class ticket? If not, please step away from the window so that I can wait on the next customer."

I was irritated, but, unless I planned on walking to Alpe-d'Huez, I needed a ticket. "Fine," I yelled loudly enough to attract the attention of a gendarme. "Give me a damn second class ticket."

I grumbled while she ran my bankcard through the machine and, then, I swiped the ticket and my receipt from the tray. As I made my way to the track, a man grabbed my arm. "Excuse me," he said. "I overheard your troubles in getting a first class ticket. Perhaps, you'd be interested in exchanging tickets with me."

I took a step backwards. Although he was dressed rather smartly, the stranger was sweating heavily. "Why would you do that?" I asked.

"I'm not feeling very well, as you can probably see," he said. "I can't get a refund for my first class ticket since I've already validated it." He pointed to the notch at the end of his ticket. "But I could get a refund for yours. You haven't validated it yet. You want to travel first class and I want my money back. It would work in both our favors."

I checked his ticket. It was for the correct train, was indeed for first class, and was in the name of "Antoine Dumas." Smiling, I happily exchanged tickets with him. "Thank you, Monsieur Dumas. Let me pay you the difference."

"No, that's not necessary," he said, already hurrying away. I found the car with my assigned seat and jumped aboard.

My seat was next to a window, facing the front. I was relieved since I got sick when I had to sit facing the rear of the train. My luck had taken a turn for the better.

In the quiet of the compartment, I felt foolish about how I treated the ticket agent. Over the course of the last several months, I had engaged in a terribly unpredictable cycle vacillating between love for my fellow man and arrogance that bordered on cruelty. There would be times when I would be "on," feeling grounded and connected and brimming with love. I would smile at strangers, seeing a soul loved by God in each of the people I crossed. But the next day could find me asserting my self-worth by refusing to budge for a pedestrian in whose path I was strolling, or honking and cursing at a driver that had the audacity of switching into my lane without signalling the move. I liked feeling the love and hated myself for feeling superior. For whatever reason, I couldn't control my attitude.

The arrival of an expensively dressed businessman terminated my self-analysis. "I believe I have the window seat," he announced.

I took a deep breath. *Love, kindness, patience*, I told myself. "I'm afraid you're mistaken. This is my seat."

He asked to see my ticket. I took a deep breath to calm myself and held my ticket in front of his face.

"I apologize," he said, then deposited his briefcase on the overhead rack and sat in the seat next to mine.

I was tempted to stretch out my legs and use the chair across from me as an ottoman when the compartment door was again opened—this time by a man about twenty years old. The businessman next to me and I did double-takes. This new arrival was not your typical first class passenger. His head was completely shaved although it was evident that he was not balding. He was dressed in torn jeans, black tee-shirt and black leather coat. He had an earring in his left ear, a stud in his nose, wore dark sunglasses and his face bore the scars of a teenage battle with acne. He plopped down across from me and began tapping his big black boots against the floor.

What in the world does he do for a living? I winced at my own thought. It wasn't a matter of curiosity. It was a way for me to put him down, to feel superior to him. I sighed. What was wrong with me? I thought that I'd learned from Christophe not to judge people based on their appearance. Part of the problem was the very same spiritual awareness that made me more loving. It also gave me a sense of superiority. Okay, I admitted, spirituality didn't make me feel superior—I chose to feel superior. Why did I have to put this kid down? Worse, why was I threatened by him?

He caught me staring and smiled. I turned my attention beyond the window.

The train was quiet, only slightly rocking. If not for the blurs outside the window, there would have been no indication that we were traveling so fast.

"Where are you headed?" the young guy asked. The businessman and I both looked up at the same time. The question was not directed at me.

The businessman glanced my way, a look of irritation in his countenance. "Alpe-d'Huez," he said quickly, then adjusted himself and snapped the newspaper open again.

"No shit?" the younger man responded. "Me, too!"

This was too bizarre.

"How about you?"

I couldn't lie. We were all going to be on the same connecting train from Grenoble. "Alpe-d'Huez," I said without any fanfare.

The businessman glanced at me, but just as quickly, returned to his newspaper. The young man's jaw had dropped to his boots. *"Putain!* What are the chances that all three of us in the same compartment would be going to the same village? I mean, the three of us are practically going to double the population," he laughed.

What *were* the chances? I wondered.

Before he could delve into the statistical probability of the coincidence, the conductor appeared outside our compartment. *"Vos billets, s'il vous plait."* I hoped he wouldn't ask for identification. I didn't want to have to explain why I was carrying a ticket assigned to someone named Antoine Dumas.

After studying our tickets, he returned them. "You're in the wrong car," he said to the young man. "You've got second class tickets. Six cars to the rear."

I, regrettably, felt relieved. For whatever reason, the young guy made me uncomfortable. The only thing I could conclude was that he was unpredictable. At least, that's what his appearance suggested to me.

He looked at us and shrugged. "Well, it was nice talking to you. See you in Alpe-d'Huez."

"Finally," my only remaining traveling companion said after our leather-clad friend had left. "A little peace and quiet."

I had considered asking the businessman if, by chance, he was going to my sister's wedding. I didn't know any of Christophe's guests. But his last comment shut me up.

I had forty minutes between trains in Grenoble. The TGV ran only along the main routes, so I would be on an older *SNCF* train for the final trek up to Alpe-d'Huez.

After buying a newspaper from the kiosk, I called Camille to tell her what train I was taking. I had wanted to surprise her, but I needed to be picked up at the train station. My itinerary established, I sat down at a table in the *Bar du Gare* and ordered a beer. I read two articles before realizing that I had yet to memorize my toast. I was walking my sister down the aisle on Saturday. While that role alone required that I toast the new couple, I was also known in the family as the toastmaster. I prided myself on never reading from a prepared text.

I had barely withdrawn my speech from my pocket when I noticed Antoine Dumas, the man who had given me his first class ticket, walking across the train station. I was watching him, wondering what he was doing in Grenoble, when someone pulled out a chair at my table. I looked over.

"Hey, there," said the young first class wannabe through a big smile.

"*Salut*," I responded, failing to return the smile. I looked back toward the atrium, but Monsieur Dumas had disappeared in the crowd.

The young man sat down. "I never got a chance to introduce myself." He extended a hand. "Michel Slugane."

Shaking his hand, I said, "*Enchanté.*"

"What's your name?"

"Eric Pétris," I mumbled.

"So, what takes you to Alpe-d'Huez?"

I lowered my toast. "My sister's wedding." I was tempted to return my attention to the toast, but decided to make a concerted effort to be kind instead of cruel and judgmental. I would have to start with my body-language. Since he'd arrived, I'd crossed my arms, crossed my legs and turned forty-five degrees away from him. I tried to loosen up and smiled.

"That's cool. I love weddings." He dropped his back-pack on the floor. "I also love Alpe-d'Huez. It's awesome in the summer."

"Hm-hm." My goal of being courteous took a blow when I noticed he had leaned back in his chair, oblivious to the fact that he was crushing my jacket.

The waiter appeared. "*Vous désirez?*" he asked, dropping a cardboard coaster in front of Michel.

He pointed to my beer. "*Une pression aussi.*" After the waiter left, Michel crossed his arms on the table, leaning closer to me. "Where's your friend?"

"Who?" I thought for a moment he was talking about the mysterious Monsieur Dumas.

"The guy you were traveling with."

"Oh," I said, shaking my head. "I'm not traveling with him. I don't even know him."

Michel seemed perplexed. "I was sure you two knew each other."

"Because we're both going to Alpe-d'Huez? No. I don't know him."

"I just figured you two knew each other from court."

I dropped the pages of the toast to my lap. "How did you know I go to court?"

"You're an attorney, right?"

I nodded. I didn't like this stranger knowing I was an attorney, especially when I had no idea who he was. "You've seen me around the courthouse?"

"That's right." He wasn't persuasive.

"What were you doing there?"

"Just hanging out. You know, observing. I saw that other guy, too."

"Strange. I don't remember you."

Michel laughed. "And you'd undoubtedly remember someone who looks like me in the *Palais de Justice*, right?"

"Well, yes," I admitted. That's exactly what I'd been thinking.

He shook his head. "I don't look like this when I'm in court. They'd throw me out."

"What do you do?"

"As in, what's my job? I don't work—at least, not in the, you know, *conventional* sense. I'm not a nine-to-five kind of guy. I'm an artist. That's what I do. Unfortunately, it doesn't pay."

"Then, how do you support yourself?"

"I get by. When I have to, I'm a handyman. I pitch in here and there, do odd jobs, barter my services. It lets me remain free to roam, to experience, to observe."

Michel's beer arrived. He raised it. "To freedom," he toasted.

We clanked glasses and I watched him over the rising rim of my glass. I was fairly certain his freedom was financed in no small part by my taxes in the form of social security and unemployment benefits. I could sense animosity towards this kid, this stranger, swelling up inside me. What was it? He hadn't done anything to me. If he took advantage of our government's generosity, why should I care? *Because he's free and you're not.* Not free in the sense of financial freedom, but free from societal constraints. That was it, I realized. I was struggling to disconnect from the tenets of society and was suffering through the process. This kid was free not just from society's tenets, but from societal constraints altogether.

He was unpredictable for the very reason that he didn't conform. The businessman in our compartment and I were predictable. We would not strike up a conversation with a stranger. We would not start humming or singing aloud. We would behave as society expected us to behave. This kid could not be trusted to "behave."

"What's that you're reading?" he asked, pointing to the paper in my hands.

"My toast for my sister and her husband-to-be."

"Cool. Do you like your future brother-in-law?"

He was proving my point. "That's a little personal."

Michel shrugged. "I guess that means no. Most people only refuse to answer when there's a problem."

"That's *not* what it means. I simply don't wish to discuss my family with someone I've just met."

"Fair enough. Do you have any kids?" He pointed to my *alliance*. "I see you're married."

"Yeah, four."

"Wow!" he said with a big grin. "You're sure getting your share, huh?"

I gathered my duffel bag and stood. "I'm going to get a seat on the train," I said. "*Bon voyage*." I wrestled my sport coat from his chair and left my beer on the table, more than half full.

I hurried down the *quai* towards the first class car. I couldn't believe the nerve of that kid. That was the problem with youth today. They had no sense of propriety, of discretion. I noticed upon boarding that the business man next to me on the TGV was already seated in the car. I chose a seat on the outside of the *quai*, just so Michel, walking down the track, wouldn't be able to see me. I hoped he was again in second class.

I was no longer feeling guilty about my negative judgments of Michel. He proved worthy. How dare he make that comment about my wife! Actually, I thought, it wasn't really about Camille. In fact, I often kidded my friends about not "getting any" after they were married. What was so wrong with Michel complimenting me for having a good sex life? Camille's words sounded in my head: "You've got to learn to chill, Eric."

I was anxious to get back to my family. It had only been a few hours, less than a full day of work, but the distance nagged at me.

A smile blossomed. It felt good to miss them. It felt good just to feel. The last seven months had been incredible. If someone had told me a year earlier that, over the course of the following year, I would finally be feeling emotion, I would be meditating, suffering no more illnesses or migraines, weep out of love for my wife, have my soul leave my body and take flight, do battle with Lucifer—"impossible" isn't a strong enough word.

The notion of heading to Marseilles was exciting. Well, the city wasn't all that attractive to us. But, Camille and I had both agreed that we'd spend two years there. Two more years, we figured, would be enough for the sale of my first book to finally occur. And the job was pretty much the same as what I was doing now.

At the same time, it was difficult to leave Pascal's firm. There could be no other employers like him. And we had a long history together. He worked for my father. Then, I worked for him. It was a family operation and he treated the firm and me as such.

The firm in Marseilles, while very successful, would be a step back for me. It was the same kind of practice of law. It was not, however, the same philosophy of practice.

What the hell! It was a change. That's what I needed. And the proof was how easy it had been to procure the job. Unemployment in France was hovering around twelve percent. Clearly, God was telling me this was the right path.

The right path... The phrase triggered something in my head. Christophe had mentioned the importance of looking for the strings that tie events together. What was today all about? I went to Lyon for, essentially, no reason. The easy answer was that I'd made a dumb mistake in saving the document in the wrong computer file, but that didn't justify the trip. There must be some grander reason why I left Alpe-d'Huez in the middle of the wedding festivities and was traveling to and from Lyon in one day. Getting Monsieur Dumas a refund was too petty a reason; certainly not worth an entire day in my life. Besides, unless I had mistaken someone else for him, he'd actually used my second class ticket. I wondered what the point was to this trip. God, I hoped it didn't have anything to do with Michel. After all, I'd been pretty rigid with him. I'd have to pay closer attention, be more vigilant. After another five minutes of searching for a meaning, I realized that, sometimes, we waste time and money on stupid mistakes. There was no universal or divine reason for this trip. I screwed up and was paying for my stupidity. With that realization, I dozed off.

When I awakened, I was on the floor of the railcar. I seemed to remember a loud crash. I was not the only one disturbed. Bags, papers and coats lined the aisle. People scrambled to right themselves and gather their belongings. I picked up my coat and duffel bag, then braced myself, as a loud screeching sound filled the train with the hard employment of the emergency brakes. After thirty seconds, the train stopped.

"What happened?" echoed throughout the car.

The windows were lowered and the passengers strained to see what had happened. The businessman from the TGV rushed by me, opened the door and jumped onto the tracks. Several others followed. I decided to stay put. Within five minutes, the car emptied as a long line of people snaked their way to the front of the train to investigate.

The first person to return was the businessman. "We hit a car," he announced with disgust.

"*Merde.*"

He nodded and made his way past me. Others began streaming in.

"Is anyone hurt?" I asked.

"No," a middle-aged woman answered. "The car was left on the tracks. There's no driver."

I noticed several people, including the businessman, gathering their affairs together. "Where is everyone going?" I asked him.

He pointed out the window. "To hitch a ride."

There was a small, two-lane road six hundred meters from the tracks, a field of wild grass separating us.

"Is the train damaged?"

"It doesn't appear to be."

"Well, how long can it take to remove the car from the tracks?"

Another man answered. "Evidently, a long time, since they're sending another train to pick us up."

The businessman huffed. "They have to wait for investigators from the SNCF, the municipal police and the *Gendarmerie Nationale* to arrive and conduct their interviews, do measurements—" He threw his hand down in disgust. "As soon as the functionaries get involved, forget it!"

"Why don't you wait for the next train?" I asked. "It's safer than hitchhiking."

"If you want to wait for another train, be my guest."

I looked out the window. At least thirty people were of the businessman's opinion and were heading towards the road.

Hitchhiking did not appeal to me, however. There had been too many stories over the last ten years of hitchhikers disappearing. While most were teenaged girls, I still preferred to wait for the next train in the comfort of the railcar versus putting my life in the hands of a complete stranger.

Ten minutes later, there were over one hundred passengers heading for the road. I was the only one left in my railcar. I was becoming uncomfortable. Maybe, the others knew more than I.

I stepped off the train. The midday sun was beating down. A human wall was now built along the *route nationale*. I decided that I wasn't going to be the only one stranded on a broken-down train. If I could just get to the next village, I would call Camille and have her or my brother pick me up. I figured it was over a two-hour ride to Alpe-d'Huez. But, the chance that another train would arrive in the next two hours seemed highly unlikely.

I began my trek across the field, surprised that the grass was higher and the ground more uneven than it appeared from the train. Up ahead, I saw that the road was not well traveled and only one in five cars was stopping. With so many hitchhikers, I worried about getting lucky enough to land a ride. I picked up my pace.

The noise of the passengers' pleading for each passing car to stop was deafening, not to mention completely out of place in the tranquil, rolling countryside. I was at the roadside no more than a minute when a tiny Austin stopped in front of me.

Michel stuck his head out the window. "Hey, Eric! You're in luck. Climb in."

I peered past Michel to the driver. He was a teenaged punk rocker, with more silver and gold in his nose, ears and lips than my wife and sisters combined. He sported a spiked mohawk that brushed the roof of the miniature car. The back seat was smaller than a large suitcase. But, I realized, beggars can't be choosy. Suddenly, I felt somebody at my side. It was the businessman.

He grunted his disgust. "Listen, if you like, you can wait five minutes." He showed me a cellular phone in his hand. "A friend of mine is on his way to pick me up and give me a lift to Alpe-d'Huez."

"*Merci,*" I said, then bent down to look in the Austin. "Thanks anyway. I'll wait."

Michel shrugged and waved to the driver to move on.

Five minutes later, the entreaties of the gathered passengers grew to a crescendo as a large black BMW sedan made its way slowly along the line of hitchhikers. It slowed and stopped in front of the businessman and me. We had to fight off the other passengers who thought the BMW was stopping at random.

I was offered the front seat. I thanked the driver and the businessman profusely and settled in on the plush leather seat.

The driver was a small, balding man. He didn't smile. He and the businessman briefly exchanged pleasantries once we left the roadside.

The big BMW purred along the route nationale at over a hundred kilometers an hour. I smiled to myself. This was actually better than the train. In fact, I estimated that I would arrive in advance of the time I had told Camille.

I turned to the driver. "It's awfully nice of you to take us all the way to Alpe-d'Huez."

"No problem at all."

"So, Antoine," the businessman in back said, "what takes you to Alpe-d'Huez? Summer vacation?"

I frowned. "Antoine?" Then, I remembered. Shaking my head, I said, "My name isn't Antoine Dumas."

"But your ticket said Antoine Dumas," the man in back quickly protested.

The driver turned and stared at me. Then, he applied the brake and turned off the *route nationale* onto a dirt road.

"Who are you?" the businessman demanded in a strangely irritated tone.

"Eric Pétris. Why?"

The man in back pulled a gun from inside his coat.

"What the hell—" I stammered. My heart was in my throat. This was surreal. I had felt so safe and fortunate just ten seconds earlier!

The driver relieved me of my duffel bag and tossed it in the back seat.

"Your coat," demanded the man with the gun.

I gave it to him without hesitation.

"Empty your pockets."

I did, turning over my keys and over two hundred francs.

The car began climbing. The man in the rear seat opened my wallet. "Eric Pétris!" he yelled. "Who the hell are you?"

"Just what it says—just what I told you. Eric Pétris."

The driver turned in astonishment. "It's probably a fake."

"I'm afraid not," said the man in back, reading one of my cards. "You're a lawyer?"

I nodded quickly. "What's going on?"

"How did you get the ticket belonging to Monsieur Dumas?"

A sick feeling struck me. "He asked to exchange tickets with me in Grenoble. I gave him my second class ticket for his first."

"Damn him!" the man in the back yelled.

"How could Dumas have known?" asked the driver.

"How the hell should I know?"

"Who is Dumas?" I asked.

The man in the back didn't respond. Instead, he dialed a number on his cellular phone. "It's me. No, we don't have Dumas. He changed seats with some lawyer and we grabbed the lawyer by mistake... Yeah, he's here now... Alright." He folded the phone in two and replaced it in his coat pocket.

"Look," I said, "this is just a mistake. Let me go and I won't—"

"Sorry," said the man in the back seat. He made eye contact with the driver and nodded.

We continued to climb for another five minutes until we were in a forest.

"What are you going to do?" I finally asked. "I have a wife and four children. I'll give you everything I have, but don't shoot me."

"You made a bad choice, Maître Pétris. You should have traveled second class." The gun remained fixed on me.

My level of anger was quickly rising to my level of fear. It was one thing to kill me, but to take away Camille's husband, to take away Marie's, Pierre's, Marc's and Cédric's father! It wasn't right. Not just in the moral sense, either. It just didn't seem possible to me. It wasn't my time to die. I turned to see where we were going. The forest was growing darker.

I couldn't allow this to happen. I had to do something. I couldn't allow myself to be driven to the slaughter without putting up a fight. My adrenaline level was exploding and I thought that if they didn't shoot me, I would die of a heart attack.

This is wrong! I kept repeating to myself. Camille's face and the faces of our children ran through my mind's eye on an endless loop. It was wrong to do this to them, and *damn it*, it was wrong to do this to me. But talking to myself was not changing my predicament.

Without thinking, without planning, I pushed open the door and spun out of the car.

I bounced hard on the embankment, then fell back into the rut of the road. Facing the way we had come, I was dizzy, in pain and disoriented. But my hearing worked fine. The BMW was skidding to a stop behind me.

Without looking, I threw myself beyond the tree line. Just as I pushed myself to my feet, a shot rang out. The bullet splintered the bark of a tree to my right. I scrambled deeper into the forest, hunched over, afraid to run upright. Ten meters, twenty, fifty, maybe, a hundred meters. I had no idea how far into the forest I had run. Nor did I know what direction I had headed. I was going so fast and dodging tree after tree, for all I knew, I could have run in a circle.

I crouched down and listened. I couldn't hear anything over the sound of my own breathing. My heart was pounding, my lungs were gasping. In my head, the sounds were loud enough to attract anyone within five kilometers of me. But I couldn't move. Without any bearings, I didn't know if my next step would put me back on the road, staring at the BMW sedan.

Fifteen minutes passed—just enough time to stop worrying so much about my assailants as about how I was going to get to civilization from where I was. The forests in the Alps were vast, unending blankets of pines. The ceiling of the forest prevented me from getting a look at the sun. I was lost—no compass, no sun to guide me. And I knew all too well that I would starve to death if I walked around in circles for days on end.

I sat down on the carpet of pine needles. My head fell forward into my hands. *How the hell did this happen to me?*

The damn SNCF—if they could run a railroad properly, this would never have happened. The driver in the BMW probably left the car on the tracks to get me out of the train, but I know it wouldn't have happened in Switzerland or Germany. They know what efficient means. The train engineer should have stopped without hitting the car. At least, the SNCF should have been more reassuring about getting another train to pick us up. They could have had buses pick us up. After all, the buses, railroad, airlines—the French government owns it all. Our fucking tax dollars at work!

And Pascal! If he wasn't such a computer illiterate, or, if someone in the office had had the common sense to make photocopies for godsakes, I wouldn't be in this mess. I never would have left Alpe-d'Huez. In fact, I'd be river-rafting right now. But, no. I'm sitting in the middle of some godforsaken forest in the middle of I don't know where, with no money, no wallet—I'm fucked! Fucked! Fucked! Fucked!

A thought made its way to the surface despite the violent storm inside me: You should have taken the ride from Michel and that punk-rocker.

I shook my head in disgust. I couldn't be sure I wouldn't have ended up in similar or worse circumstances. That conclusion caused mental indigestion. Michel might not have been the kind of person with whom I would choose to socialize, but he was not dangerous. There was absolutely nothing threatening about him. At least not in a physical way. He may threaten my sense of what is proper dress or comportment, but he was no threat to my life.

What was threatening about the guy in the suit? I wondered. Nothing, really. He was well dressed, well polished—he appeared wealthy. His friend drove a BMW sedan. *That was it, wasn't it? Face it, Eric, you liked how the guy looked. Your gut never got a chance to react to him one way or the other, because your brain was telling you— that's the kind of guy you can trust. Anyone who dresses that well, is clean shaven, and smells of money must be safe.*
Idiot!

I had done the same thing with Christophe. His long hair, earrings, and that come-what-may attitude were the limits of my investigation. I had written him off based on a picture Elisabeth brought home. Judgment against the young defendant based solely on a picture. I'd done the same thing all over again with Michel. The worst part was that I realized it while it was happening. I knew I was a jerk in the cafe. I knew I had treated him badly. Taking the ride with him would have been an opportunity to make up for it. But I chose the well-dressed forty year-old and the BMW over the punk twenty year-olds and the tiny Austin. *And you call yourself Catholic!* I was ashamed of myself. That mentality had gotten me into trouble—almost killed. I wondered, with all of my work and progress in cultivating my spiritual side—love, intuition, nonphysical communication—why was I still judging people based on appearances?

I was a snob. Not only did I base my judgment of people on appearances, but I judged myself that way, too. I was too good to travel second class. I *had* to have a first class seat.

Idiotic snob!

As the thought left me, bouncing off of several tree trunks, I started to laugh. I had become complacent again. And my damn angel wouldn't allow that to last too long. This was another lesson from my winged mentor. I laughed harder. My angel had style, I had to admit. And when he wanted to screw with me, he was the king of court jesters.

I wished he'd make himself seen.

"This isn't funny," I yelled at the treetops. "I almost got killed. A whisper, maybe even a knock on the head would have sufficed, don't you think? Were gunshots really necessary?"

A honk in the distance startled me. I swore at myself for yelling when I had no idea whether the men in the BMW had given up their search. "Help me," I pleaded to my angel, slightly less vociferously than my last communication.

The honk rang through the trees again. Its noise was tinny. It didn't sound like the horn of a BMW. But I had no intention of staking my life on my ability to differentiate between car horns.

"Eric!" a voice called out. "Eric!"

Damn it, I thought. It had to be the guys in the BMW. They had my wallet and my *carte d'intentité*.

"Eric!"

It didn't sound like the guy with the gun. *It could be the driver*, I thought.

"Eric!"

I recognized the voice. It sounded like Michel.

"Eric! *C'est Michel.* Are you out there?"

It *was* Michel. I followed his voice until I could see the little Austin through the trees. It was parked on the same road from which I'd escaped minutes earlier. Still nervous, I hid and waited.

"Eric!" Michel called from my left.

I waited until he made his way back to the car. He and the punk rocker that picked him up started talking.

"I've gotta get going," the driver said.

"Please, just five more minutes," Michel asked.

"Maybe he was in the BMW."

"We both saw it come back down this road. There was nobody in the front passenger seat."

"If you want to stay, that's fine, but I've gotta go."

I came out from behind the trees.

"There he is!" Michel yelled, smiling as if he'd found a long lost brother. "Are you alright, Eric?"

"I'm fine. What are you doing here?"

"He convinced me to double back to see if you'd had second thoughts about a ride," the punk rocker explained, his arms crossed, a snarl on his face.

Michel shrugged. "You were getting into that big BMW just as we went by. We made a U-turn, and, when we saw you pull off the *route nationale*, we were curious and followed."

"I can't tell you how happy I am that you did." Unable to bridle my gratitude, I threw my arms around him and hugged him. "Thank you. You saved my life!"

"What happened?"

I checked the road for any sign of the black sedan. "Let's get out of here. I'll tell you on the way."

We were puttering along the *route nationale*. The car was moving at only eighty kilometers an hour, but by the scream of the little engine and the deafening rattling of the car's body, it seemed like we were about to break the sound barrier. I smiled to myself. My angel was really on a roll—different example, but the same lesson. Despite the appearance of the car and my two traveling companions, I wouldn't have changed places with someone in a luxury sedan at that moment for all the money in the world.

My audience was spellbound by the story of what happened to me in the BMW. Several times, I had to tell the driver to stop watching me in the rearview mirror and concentrate on the road.

"Did you get the license plate number?"

I rolled my eyes. "Are you kidding? I was lucky to get away alive."

Michel shook his head in shock, then, turned to the front. I wasn't sure, but I thought I saw him make the sign of the cross.

We pulled into a little village called Livet. It was as far as our chauffeur was headed. I was reluctant to leave the Austin, wondering whether that big black car was going to come around the corner at any second. On the other hand, I seriously doubted whether the Austin could manage to climb any farther up the Alps with all three of us aboard.

I filed a complaint and full report with the local police. Michel proved to have an excellent eye for detail. He gave the police a much better description of the man that had been on the train while I described the driver. I explained the whole sequence of events: from Antoine Dumas's offer of his ticket to my assailants' realization that I wasn't Antoine Dumas. After the police were satisfied that they had all the information they needed, they requested my address in Alpe-d'Huez and allowed us to leave. Michel and I made for the *tabac*. While a *tabac* obviously sells tobacco products, it also is the local purveyor of phone cards. I was at the counter before I remembered that I had no money and no bank cards.

"Michel, can you loan me sixty francs for a phone card? I'll pay you back as soon as we get to Alpe-d'Huez."

Without a moment's hesitation, he pulled a pouch from his backpack. His fingers danced around inside, then, a pained expression came across his face. "All I've got is twenty-nine francs and thirty centimes."

I turned to the woman behind the counter. "Is there a phone around here that still takes coins?"

"Down the street, in front of the *pharmacie.*"

After alerting Camille that I was going to get a ride directly to the house, Michel and I found a taxi willing to take us all the way to Alpe-d'Huez. Fortunately, before departing, the taxi driver did not ask for proof that we could pay the fare.

Michel and I stretched out on the back seat. I realized how exhausted I was. I looked over at him. I wanted to reach out and hug him again. He'd saved my life. Why?

"Can I ask you something?"

He smiled. "What?"

"I was rude to you—both in the train station in Grenoble and when you offered me a ride. Why did you still want to help me?"

His smile dissipated. He seemed unsure of himself for the first time all day. "It's no big deal."

"No big deal?" I said in shock. "I could have died up there if you hadn't come back."

He shrugged.

I gave up trying to impress upon him what a jerk I'd been and what a saint he'd been. "You mentioned you were observing court proceedings the other day. Why? It's boring."

"Nothing better to do."

The lawyer in me awakened. That was a halfhearted answer if I'd ever heard one. "Which proceeding were you observing?"

He appeared confused. "I don't remember."

"Do you remember what kind of case it was?"

He shook his head.

"Let's see. The only cases I've had to appear in court for in the last week were a burglary case and a fraud case. Which one was it?"

"Burglary, I think."

"I see." I remained quiet, waiting for him to supply me with more fodder. Either he sensed that I was dubious, or, he simply didn't want to lie anymore.

"Actually," he said, "I wasn't completely truthful with you earlier."

"I know you didn't see me in court, since I handle only civil matters, not criminal."

Michel shook his head. "I didn't see you in court."

"So, how do you know me?"

He looked to see if the driver was listening to our conversation. I couldn't imagine it possible over the music blaring from the radio.

"You wouldn't believe me if I told you."

"Michel, after what happened today, I'd believe anything."

He raised his eyebrows as if to say, *Don't be so sure.* "I had a dream."

I waited. Nothing more. "And?"

He exhaled long and deeply. "I dreamt about you and that guy that was sitting next to you on the TGV. I saw you get into a big black car together. Then, I saw him try to shoot you. That's why, when I was talking to you in the bar, I thought you two knew each other."

I don't know if my jaw was on my lap or if my eyes rolled back inside my skull. It was the strangest sensation of complete astonishment and total understanding. I was flabbergasted, but I nevertheless knew every word to be true.

"In my dream, I was told that I had to get you safely to Alpe-d'Huez. Crazy, huh?"

"Uhh ... uh ... Crazy? Yes and no. Were you told why you had to save me?"

"No, but I saw a picture of the earth—you know, like those photos taken from outer space."

"What could that mean?"

He shrugged. "No idea."

I scratched my head. "So, then, how did you know I was a lawyer?"

"In my dream, that guy called you, 'Maître Pétris.'"

I had reached the point of brain-lock. I simply couldn't digest all that Michel was telling me.

"Can I ask you a question?"

Laughing, I answered, "I think I owe you at least that."

He smiled, but then, his faced changed. He looked sad. "What made you jump from that car?"

"Survival instinct, I guess."

He chewed on my answer for a minute. "Nothing was going through your mind? You just jumped?"

I leaned against the car window. "Sure, my mind was going at the speed of light. I was scared shitless. I knew in my gut they were going to kill me. At first, I was paralyzed with fear. But, then, the whole thing seemed so preposterous. I started getting angry. After all, they wouldn't just be killing me, they'd be making my wife a widow and my children fatherless. That really pissed me off. All I could think about were my wife and children. It was like they were harming them more than me. I had to do something. I couldn't just let that happen without fighting back. Can you understand?"

Michel had a far-off stare.

"Is anything wrong?"

He snapped out of his dreamlike state. "Huh?"

"Are you okay?"

He nodded quickly. "Sure."

"Why do you think you had that dream?"

He smiled. "Obviously, to save your ass."

I laughed. "Stupid question. Do you have any idea about the dream's origin?"

"Origin?"

I held up my hands. "Well, I don't think we can call it a coincidence. So, what do you think was the source of your dream? I mean, are you clairvoyant?"

Michel intertwined his fingers behind his neck and leaned back on the seat. "I never believed in God before, but ... I don't know. Maybe, I am psychic."

"Ever had a dream like this before?"

Staring at the roof of the car, he shook his head.

"For what it's worth, I do believe in God. What's more, I believe in angels. I believe that we each have an angel—one of God's soldiers—to protect, guide and train us. I think that my angel and your angel got together and picked you, for some reason, to save me today."

Michel turned away and stared out the window. I thought I'd overstepped the bounds. He seemed angry. Angry or incredulous that he had saved someone as weird as I. But, then, he sniffed. Keeping his head turned away from me, he wiped his eyes with his hands.

"Are you okay?"

He didn't respond. Not even a nod. For the rest of the ride to Alpe-d'Huez, he remained facing the window. I couldn't be sure, but he seemed to be crying. It was clear he wanted to be alone in his thoughts and I had to muster every bit of discipline and compassion to remain silent. Instead, I concentrated on sending him white light.

My meditations had become a combination of prayer to God, my guardian angel and the souls in heaven, and an invitation to God's grace. What Elisabeth had first described as white light, I later understood to be God's love. Consequently, during meditations, I would send my spirit up to God in the form of a seagull, ask for God's white light, and then my spirit would ride the wave of light back down to my body. I would relay the white light from me to those whom I loved or knew needed assistance. At the same time, I asked God to directly send that person grace, thereby creating a triangle of white light—from God to the person and to me, and from me to the person.

I closed my eyes in the back of the taxi and engaged in such a triangle of light. Perhaps because I was unable to get grounded in the moving vehicle, perhaps because of the power of the day, or perhaps because of the proximity of Michel, a very special person, when I opened my eyes, I saw the energy. We were engulfed in a sphere of shimmering, translucent light.

Christophe's admonition against being linear came back to me. The notion that Michel had a dream for the sole purpose of saving my life was too one-dimensional. There were other reasons. I had to accept that conclusion without knowing what the reasons were, because I knew at that moment that Michel needed his silence and God's white light more than I needed an explanation.

The wedding festivities were put on hold to allow for my story of danger and terror in the French Alps, and to allow for everyone in the family to gather themselves. The reactions ran the gamut from the shock and terror of Camille to the envy and admiration of my younger brother. There were demands that I go again to the police, that we change the locks at the house in Alpe-d'Huez and at the condo in Lyon, that we hire security for the wedding, that we contact an uncle who worked at the *Gendarmerie Nationale*, and that we, for the first time since my parents built the mountain retreat, engage the alarm system. I tried to assure everyone that it was a crime of opportunity and that my assailants didn't know me, let alone have a vendetta against me. The one good piece of advice—counsel that I'd forgotten since leaving the police station in Livet—was to cancel my bank card.

My brother walked over to the bar, commenting, "The good news is that you're alive and nobody got hurt. But, if I'd been in your shoes, those two would have ended up in the hospital." I laughed, although part of me believed him. He was my height, but outweighed me by more than thirty kilos.

"And the even better news," Christophe added, "is that the river rafting was canceled today because the rapids were too strong. We're going tomorrow."

That news brought an even bigger smile to my face. When my brother slipped a gin and tonic into my hand, the smile threatened to tear apart my cheeks.

Two hours later, I thought I was losing my grip on reality. It didn't seem possible. There I was, standing in a bar, the site of Christophe's bachelor party, drinking and laughing, when that same afternoon I had been looking down the barrel of a gun. I had invited Michel to join our gathering, but he never showed.

The theme of Elisabeth's and Christophe's wedding was love. While not a revolutionary theme for a wedding, they took it to heart, infusing their own love into the gathering, and creating a celebration of love. As part of their plan, they had decided to invite couples. There were naturally boyfriends and girlfriends of their friends and families whom Elisabeth or Christophe did not like. But, to be true to their theme, every invitee was urged to bring a guest.

Most of their friends were acquaintances from the University in Aix-en-Provence. When the men arrived en masse at the bar, my brother and I looked at each other like we had just walked in on the wrong party. We knew none of them.

A tall blond guy made his way towards us. His crew cut and build made him a perfect candidate for an Army recruiting poster, especially since military service was no longer mandatory in France.

"Eric and Thomas, right?" he asked, a meaty hand waiting for a shake.

We nodded.

"We're cousins!"

My brother and I looked at each other. "Excuse me," I said.

"I'm Mattieu Pétris," he said.

We laughed. Elisabeth had mentioned that one of her friends shared our family name. We exchanged greetings and he sat down. He was a pilot in the French military, currently on furlough. Anyone who didn't know us would have thought we were lifelong friends. That was true of just about all of Christophe's and Elisabeth's college friends. They were genuine people. And, they were a lot of fun.

Almost two hours into the night, I realized that Mattieu and his friends with whom I'd been speaking fit a pattern. They were the most clean-cut, sharply dressed, guys in the crowd. Guys I would call "respectable." In this case, I was right. Earlier that day, I had been dangerously wrong. I figured I should make an attempt to mingle and meet some of Elisabeth's and Christophe's other friends. I was about to get up when René happened by. I said hello and followed him out of my cocoon.

René, like all of Elisabeth's and Christophe's friends, brought a guest to the wedding. René and Philippe were the only single-sex couple there. René also happened to be Elisabeth's one friend from the University whom I had previously met—before he had come out of the closet. Upon arriving at his table just off the dance floor, he introduced me to Philippe.

After sitting down with them, it dawned on me that this was the first time I'd ever met an openly gay couple. If my friends from school could see me now, they wouldn't recognize me. I had been a boisterous voice against anything and everything gay on campus—gay rights, gay socials, gay parades, etc. The problem now was acting natural in a new and strange situation .

The last time I had seen René was during his legal studies. It was as good a place as any to start a conversation. "So, René, are you practicing now?"

He nodded while taking a puff. "Mostly corporate work. *Very* boring. Are you still at your dad's firm?"

"Yes." I was stuck. Where was I supposed to go with the conversation? I may have been trying to be cool, but I was uncomfortable regardless. I didn't want them to know I was making an effort.

René saved me temporarily. "Elisabeth told me you were moving."

"Yeah, Camille and I are heading to Marseilles."

"To do what? Still in the law?"

"Same kind of law, in fact."

"Terrific."

Another silence ensued. I looked at Philippe. He had turned away from the table as soon as we shook hands. He was obviously uncomfortable—even more so than I.

"Philippe, is this the first time you're meeting René's friends from Aix?"

With raised eyebrows, he nodded.

"Me, too. Actually, René is the only person I'd met." No reaction.

I ordered another round and had to smile. Fortunately, nobody asked me why I was smiling. But, there I was, feeling uncomfortable in my attempt to force a stilted conversation, afraid that they'd know what awful thoughts I had once harbored towards all homosexuals without even having met one. And there was Philippe, knowing nobody but Elisabeth and Christophe, meeting all of René's old friends for the first time—friends who had known René only as a heterosexual. One of us had a right to be uncomfortable and it wasn't I.

"What do you do?" I asked Philippe.

"I work in a home for retarded adults."

I grimaced. "That's got to be pretty tough—emotionally, I mean."

"Sometimes. But, it's very rewarding, too."

René shook his head. "Sometimes?" He turned to me. "He's a wreck half the time."

"What exactly do you do?"

"Teach them skills they can use to be independent. That's the goal—to teach them to live on their own."

"Do you have a pretty good success rate?"

"It really depends on the individual." Philippe turned away again.

I knew he was not trying to be rude. He was just too nervous to carry on a conversation. René seemed to read my thoughts.

"He's a little on edge," he whispered.

I smiled. "That's understandable."

René nodded. "Let me ask you something. You've been practicing law for a while, right?"

"Six years."

"Do you ever get fed up with it? Because I feel like I should be doing something else. No offense, but it's so mindless. And when I look at the partners who've been around for thirty years, they look like zombies. Plus, they're so bitter. Their only interest in you is how many hours you billed last month."

"What's your question?"

"Is it that way for you? Do you enjoy the practice?"

"I can't say that I've ever been very passionate about the law. Sometimes, with a good case, I get really involved. The thing that's made it enjoyable, for me at least, is the people I work with. Pascal DeLorier and his brother are unique. They're intelligent, generous and kind. But most importantly, we're working for the same reason— it's a means to an end. We don't work just for the sake of working. Pascal and I would rather be with our families, and he isn't afraid to admit it. Plus, he makes sure I'm with my family as much as possible.

"But I'm the exception to the rule. Most law firms are like yours. They're factories. Only, the workers wear suits instead of overalls."

René rubbed his forehead. Reaching for his cigarettes, he said, "I'm afraid that if I don't get out, I'll get immune to all the bullshit. You know, just keep rolling along from paycheck to paycheck until I'm numb. Next thing I know, I'll be fifty-five, a partner, and wondering what the hell happened to me."

"Why don't you leave?"

"See, that's the problem. I don't know what else I should be doing."

"What do you want to do?"

"I don't know."

René was genuinely frustrated and worried. I slapped him on the shoulder and smiled. "Take it easy. As long as you keep asking yourself why you're doing it, and what else you could be doing—what else you *want* to do—you won't get trapped."

"Yeah, but I don't know what else—"

"René, stop. You don't have to know tonight. And just because you don't know tonight doesn't mean you won't know when you wake up tomorrow. The key is to never stop looking. When you get complacent, that's when it's time to worry. If you stay awake, you'll know when you're supposed to know."

He nodded slowly. "Yeah, that's true."

The local band finally took a break and the D.J. played something that had a beat. Phillipe grabbed René's hand.

"Let's dance."

"Thanks for the advice," René said, crushing his cigarette. "You've saved me ten thousand francs worth of therapy."

I watched them walk to the dance floor. Maybe I imparted good advice to René, maybe not. Maybe he was just being kind. But the conversation—albeit short and stilted—did me a world of good. His questions made me think more about what I was doing in moving to Marseilles. More importantly, it reinforced what my angel had been trying to teach me.

I thought the problem was that I made judgments based on appearances. The real problem was that I made judgments at all. It was one thing to feel danger in my gut. When intuition tells you somebody intends you harm, you have to listen, or, suffer the consequences. It's an entirely different matter when you judge other people's worth. I had gone out of my way in my younger days to disparage and criticize homosexuals, liberals, atheists and any other group that did not conform to my notions of right and true. Confrontations had even escalated to fights. It was one thing to *discuss* or *debate* right and wrong and universal truths. But who the hell was I to approve or disapprove of the two men whose table I shared that evening. Who the hell was I to judge anyone? Both René and Phillipe were kind, big-hearted people.

Both could teach me a lot. Both were human beings with a soul. I wondered how many Renés and Philippes I'd missed meeting and learning from over the past thirty-one years. Well, it was too late to change that. But not too late to learn from it.

As I sat there watching them dance, I was happy. It was not pride for not having judged them as I would have a few years before. I was proud of myself because I felt love for them. And with the love, I could feel my soul expanding.

I looked around at the patrons in the bar. These were not cosmopolitan types. They were rural farmers and *paysans.* Their eyes were glued to René and Philippe and the disdain was visible. I laughed to myself. It would only be fitting that, if it came to blows tonight, I would be defending a homosexual couple after I had delivered so many spiritual blows to similarly innocent people over the years.

My guardian angel evidently thought I'd had enough for one day, and the evening ended without incident.

❀   ❀   ❀

The next morning, with the groom-to-be suffering from a substantial hangover, twenty of us were supposed to set out for our river-rafting expedition. I, however, had forgotten that I'd promised Pierre and Marc that we would go fishing on Thursday. I was awakened by two slaps in the face with a fishing pole.

I peeled open my eyes to see the excited faces of my two sons, naked, fishing poles upside down in their hands, yelling, "Ready to go fishing, dad?"

We headed for a well-known lake thirty minutes from our house. Angélique had insisted on going with us, although I knew she would last ten minutes, at most. Also along for our expedition were my brother-in-law, Antoine and his son, Daniel.

We arrived at the pristine lake, nestled at the bottom of a valley like Earl Grey in a tea cup. The children poured out of the car and scrambled to the water's edge, their fathers trailing behind, loaded with the fishing gear, cameras and snacks. The snacks had been a wise addition at the direction of our wives.

While the children jumped anxiously up and down, Antoine and I tried to corral them away from the water and untangle the lines. Once we baited the hooks and cast them in disparate spots, we relaxed. The respite lasted all of thirty seconds. The children did not grasp the notion of waiting for the fish to take the bait. In fact, unless asleep, they were incapable of remaining motionless. Each of them, as soon as the fishing pole was in hand, began reeling in the line. It became a race. Antoine and I ran from one child to the next, recasting, and recasting ad infinitum.

Quickly, the children became irritated that they weren't catching anything. Their disappointment outweighed their need to move. They reluctantly agreed to just hold the pole and wait for a bite.

Our lack of success was not due to a paucity of fish. They were literally jumping out of the water. As soon as one would break the surface, the children converged on the spot. The natural result was a tangled web of fishing lines, hooks caught in the grass and, in one case, Antoine's shirt.

"I don't want to fish anymore," Angélique announced.

One down, three to go. That's what Antoine and I were thinking. Despite the work involved, it was heaven on earth. The children were outside. It was glorious weather—dry heat, sunshine, and not a cloud in the sky. The outline of the mountains against the blue backdrop was spectacular. The meadows and forests were reflected off the surface of the pure water, disturbed only when the fish broke the surface, their ripples rolling gently to where we stood, as if to say, "Hello. Thanks for coming. But I'm not going to play with you today."

I caught Angélique and Pierre wandering away. "Where do you two think you're going?"

"To look for frogs!" Pierre said with wide eyes.

"I'll make sure Pierre doesn't fall in," Angélique said, putting her arm around her brother's shoulders.

"Oh, yeah? And who's going to make sure you don't fall in?"

Angélique shrugged. "My angel." She said it very matter-of-factly. But I was overwhelmed. It was the first sign that she trusted me. It was the first time she admitted anything about her relationship with an angel.

"Don't go near the water," I insisted nevertheless. I knew Pierre was no angel when it came to finding trouble. He wouldn't be able to resist if he had a shot at pushing Angélique into the lake.

Five minutes passed. Marc and his cousin had resumed their cycle of reeling in, asking dad to cast, reeling in ...

There had been no noise from my two oldest. I was happy that I hadn't heard any splashes, but I knew from experience that there was such a phenomenon as *too* quiet, no matter how badly Camille and I craved a break from the constant commotion that our four created.

I crept around a clump of bushes and saw Angélique and Pierre sitting on the other side of a stretch of reeds. I approached quietly from behind. Just because I had told them to be careful did not mean that I couldn't try to scare them into falling in the water.

No more than two meters away from them, I stopped. They still hadn't heard me. The ground was uneven and I got down on all fours. They weren't talking. It was too quiet and I waited.

Pierre turned to Angélique. "Tell me what it's like. I'm starting to forget."

"What?"

Pierre looked up to the sky. "What it's like up there."

"Can't you go up there any more?"

Pierre shook his head. "Only at night time, when I sleep."

My heart was in my throat. I couldn't breathe. Not only was I taken aback with what I was hearing, but I felt dirty intruding upon this conversation. If they saw me lurking behind them, I could only imagine what awful things they would think of me. But, I was frozen in place.

Angélique put her arm around Pierre and pulled his head to her shoulder. "You can still go up there if you want."

"No," he said. "I try, but I can't. And I'm forgetting what it's like."

"It's very beautiful. There are angels everywhere. And *la Vièrge Marie* lets you sit on her lap."

"What color are the angels?"

"They're all different colors. They're all girls. They have big, white wings and long hair. They sing all the time."

"They're very nice?"

"Mhmm. They're very, very nice."

I wanted to sit down next to them. I wanted Angélique to talk more about what it's like up there. But I knew I wasn't supposed to be part of this conversation. I was meant to hear it, but not partake. Between what I was hearing and my own meditations during which I brought white light in through the top of my head, I began wondering if a baby's fontanel wasn't a symbol for an infant's initial openness to God, then, slowly closing as the child learns to operate in the limited world we have created for ourselves. There wasn't time to ponder the matter. I didn't want to be caught eavesdropping.

I backed up with excruciatingly slow movements. About three meters from them, I stood up and shouted, "There you are. What are you doing?"

"Looking at the clouds," said Angélique.

I looked up. "There are no clouds."

"Yes, there are. You just can't see them, Daddy."

We returned to my mother's house famished, with no fish and four yawning children. There were two surprises awaiting me. The police had found and arrested my two friends in the black BMW. A note at the front door indicated that they had also recovered my wallet and *carte d'indentité,* and that both were available at the police station for my retrieval. Even more exciting was a note left by Michel.

Dear Eric,

I told you at the end of my dream I saw the earth as if I was in outer space. What God was trying to show me was that the world is round. You thought that I was chosen to save your life. Well, you were chosen to save mine, too. Tuesday night, before I fell asleep and had the dream about you, I tried to kill myself. I stole a bottle of sleeping pills from my sister's apartment and swallowed whatever was left. When I woke up, I couldn't understand why I was alive, looked at the bottle and realized that the pills were over eight years old. I figured there must have been a reason, so I went to the *Gare Part-Dieu* to find you. The reason was that you had the answer I had been looking for. You jumped from that car instead of letting them hurt or kill you. You told me you did it because of your wife and children. They are the meaning in your life. Now, I know I have to find a meaning in my life. I don't know what it is yet, but I know in my heart that there is one. Otherwise, I would never have had that dream. Now, I also believe in angels. Thank your angel for me for saving my life.

Your friend, Michel.

I sat down on the patio wall, my eyes searching the sky in terror. The letter fell from my shaking hands. I should have been happy or proud or thankful. But, I was terrified. I was more frightened than when I'd been in the black BMW, a pistol pointed at me. *What if? What if Michel hadn't come back for me? I was rude enough as it was; what if I'd been as rude as I intended and Michel said, "The hell with him."? What if I'd screwed up God's plan and Michel ended up trying to kill himself again?* The near-miss scared the shit out of me. I had done just about everything to get rid of Michel. I'd been rude, a snob, cruel. I had tried to derail God's plan without knowing what God's plan was. *Jesus! How was I supposed to know?*

Christophe saw me, pale and shaking, sitting outside. "What's up?" he asked, joining me.

"Have you ever narrowly missed a deadly car accident?"

"Couple of times."

"You know that sickening feeling in your stomach right after you're safe? That's what I'm feeling right now."

After I explained what I'd learned about Michel, Christophe rocked back and forth, his hands clasped between his knees. "When you were in that car, were you hoping for some kind of help?"

"Absolutely. I was praying like crazy."

"Did you imagine Michel when you were hoping for help?"

I laughed. "He was the farthest thing from my mind. Although, I did wish I had accepted his offer of a ride."

"What kind of help did you imagine?"

"I don't know. A police blockade. A lightning bolt from heaven that would knock the two guys out."

"But your help came from Michel."

"Yeah, not at all what I expected."

"Do you think he was the answer to your prayers?"

"He definitely was. I just made the mistake of not looking for the extraordinary in the ordinary."

Chris smiled. "How about your refusal to accept the situation in Lyon and travel second class?"

"What about it?"

"Well, you wouldn't have been mistaken for that other guy, right?"

"Yeah."

"Do you think there was a reason first class happened to be sold-out today?"

"To save my ass. Or, maybe so that I would have met Michel and been forced to spend time with him."

"Why were you so against traveling second class?"

"Because it's not as nice as first." I laughed. "Because I'm a snob."

"So?"

"Sometimes the right choice is the simple thing instead of the fancy thing. God seems to prefer to work where there are less material distractions, huh?"

"True. But there's something else. In order for something dangerous or bad to be tempting, it has to be draped in cool, glittery packaging."

"Right, but while a gift might not have any pretty wrapping or bows, you at least know what you're getting."

Christophe stared at me for a few seconds, then left me to contemplate my lesson alone.

✻   ✻   ✻

That night, after dinner, we sat out on the patio at my mother's house. Clouds had moved into the valley. Elisabeth, two of our sisters, Christophe, Pierre and I sat outside talking. Elisabeth pulled Pierre onto her lap.

"You know Christophe and I are getting married, right?"

Pierre nodded. "When I'm big, I'm going to get married, too. I'm going to have two wives."

We laughed. "Why two wives?" his aunt asked.

Pierre shrugged. "I don't know," he said with a goofy grin.

"You know, Pierre, we're going to move away from Lyon and we won't see you as often anymore?"

"Why?"

Elisabeth smiled. "Because we want to live somewhere else. Just like you and your family. You're moving to a new place because that's where you want to live. But, we love you. And no matter where we are, we'll always love you."

"I love you, too." His blue eyes twinkled under sun-bleached blond hair.

Elisabeth hugged him. "You're so cute!"

"No, *you're* so cute," he said, enjoying the laughter he was getting.

"You know, even though we won't be living in the same place, we can still talk on the phone. You can call me anytime. And I want you to do something for me."

"What?"

"I want you to pray for me."

"I've got an idea. How about if, at night, you go see Baby Jesus and we can talk."

Elisabeth looked over Pierre's head at me. She stroked his hair. "What do you mean?"

"At night, I go up and see Baby Jesus. If you come too, we could talk. Okay?"

Elisabeth, a tear in her eye, kissed Pierre's forehead. "Definitely. That's a great idea."

I sat back in my chair, staring at my son. I was beginning to understand. Angélique, and Pierre until recently, could access the supernatural—the spiritual realm—at any time. But, now, Pierre was beginning to forget how to do it while he was conscious and was limited to seeing angels and Baby Jesus while he slept. I couldn't help but conclude that it was, at least partly, my fault. It wasn't that I had openly declared such matters impossible or ridiculous. But I had limited myself. And children do more than just observe us with their senses; they observe much deeper. *If Daddy doesn't recognize "that place up there," then we shouldn't.*

A few drops sprinkled the table and our heads. We gathered up the remaining glasses and playing cards and ran inside the house. I remained at the door, looking out. It was warm despite the rain. I was not ready to sleep. I was not ready to give up the fresh air.

Elisabeth arrived at my side. "What are you thinking? About Pierre?"

"Actually, I was thinking that I don't want to stay inside." I smiled. "Want a beer?"

"Sure," she said. "Where are you going?"

I ran to the refrigerator, pulled out two beers, grabbed Pierre's hand and ran out in the rain, Elisabeth chasing after us. We got soaked on our way to the jungle-gym in the back of the house. There were three swings along the length of the apparatus, then a slide that came down from an elevated platform with a tent above it. Under the tent, we took refuge from the rain. Within two minutes, Christophe and my two other sisters followed.

The six of us, our legs entangled, water dripping off us and pounding the canvas roof above our heads, laughed with abandon. Pierre, happy to be with five kids, talked as if his sentence of silence had just been commuted.

"God, I'm happy to be part of this family," Christophe said.

"We're the better for it," I responded. "And I'm *much* better for it." With that, I went down the slide and jumped on a swing. The jungle-gym was old and unaccustomed to an adult's weight. The platform swayed with each thrust of the swing. Pierre wasted no time in joining me. He did not want to swing by himself. Instead, he climbed onto my lap so that we were facing each other. Swinging with my son, our backs arched, mouths open to collect the rain—it was a magical moment.

"Pierre, when you're seventeen," my sister called out, "and you don't think your dad is cool, I hope you remember this."

I wasn't worried about what Pierre thought of me when he was seventeen. I didn't even worry about tomorrow. Too often in the past I'd had a brief moment of joy, love, kindness, or honesty, only to return to my bitter, myopic ways the following day, like a man who wakes up with a hangover, more pained by the truthfulness of his words and actions the preceding night than by his headache. But not me. Not anymore. I was going to enjoy the moment—inebriated only with love and joy. Yesterday was useless, tomorrow wasn't guaranteed. All I had was that moment. It was all I wanted.

❀   ❀   ❀

As my soul expanded, so did my capacity to love. It was extraordinary. I was even feeling love for strangers I'd pass in the street. A large part of it was the love that surrounded me in Alpe-d'Huez, but the change began back in Lyon. There was simply more room in my heart and less clutter between my spirit and the physical world around me. My relationship with my children was the best evidence of this change. I also noticed how my increased capacity to love protected me. I never would have imagined such a thing possible; but there was no doubt that, as I directed more and more of my energy towards positive thoughts and feelings, the by-product of love was protection from other people's negativity, even cruelty. On Friday afternoon in Alpe-d'Huez, shortly before the rehearsal dinner, I was able to combine my new relationship with my children with my new understanding of the power of love.

Marc and Pierre were playing on the jungle-gym in the back yard. I was ten meters away, practicing my toast. I looked up in time to see Marc connect with a roundhouse to Pierre's cheek.

"Daddy!" Pierre yelled. "Marc hit me."

"Tell him you love him, Pierre," I said without thinking.

My oldest son looked at me, not surprisingly confused. "No, daddy. Marc hit *me*."

"I know. Tell Marc that you love him."

His forehead wrinkled with a frown, Pierre pointed to himself. "*Me* tell Marc?"

"That's right."

Pierre shrugged. "Marc, I love you."

"I love you, too, Pierre."

There was no more fighting that afternoon. I wish I could report that there was no further fighting at all, but that's not the case. Nevertheless, every time one of the children was hurt, offended or suffered, I told him or her to say, "I love you." It converted the erstwhile victim into the one with the power. I was initially worried that they'd figure out the pattern and the assailant would take advantage of the other's "turn the other cheek" posture. While they did figure out the pattern, and began saying, "I love you" without my instruction, the wrong-doer immediately ceased his or her behavior. Each time, the expression of love provided a brief detente among my little combatants.

Perhaps one day, I'll have the courage to tell everyone who tries to harm me, "I love you." It would certainly lead to a different world.

❈   ❈   ❈

When Camille, our children and I returned to Lyon, there was something very, very wrong. There was an emptiness. Certainly, we missed Elisabeth and Christophe, but that wasn't it. It was anticlimactic returning to our condo after the festivities. Their wedding day was pure energy. From the morning through the last dance, we were in another world. Christophe was in tears until a few minutes before the ceremony. His father called him to convey his pride, opening the floodgates of Christophe's eyes. The ponytailed young man with the appropriately equine-sized heart thanked us for sharing in "the greatest day of my life." The newlyweds had written personalized letters to each guest that marked our places at the dinner table, the reading of which ignited another explosion of tears. The toasts were exquisite—each one straight from the speaker's heart. Light from over one hundred candles danced among us. And Father Brion's sermon was worth the wait. He reminded us that love takes work, that it's a choice we make each and every day. When I spoke to him at the reception, I understood that he knew before I did what awaited me that week, both in terms of trials and lessons, in terms of love and expansion of the soul. But even the letdown after the incredible wedding couldn't be blamed for the terrible funk we were suffering.

I didn't have much time to contemplate what was bothering me. The day after our return, I left for Marseilles for a meeting with my future firm—a meeting to introduce me to the associates and partners I had not yet met. I looked forward to the trip and I wasn't disappointed. The sun was shining on the Riviera as I drove down the *Autoroute du Soleil*. The temperature was tropical and the Mediterranean was beckoning. There was little traffic and I arrived in Marseilles more than two hours before my meeting. I found a parking spot just in front of a café which was across *La Canebière* from a five-story office building, the top floor of which the firm occupied.

I ordered a coffee and *croque monsieur* at a sidewalk table and looked out onto Marseille's main street.

My nerves were calm. I had no trouble eating. I wasn't running through scenarios of how this meeting with my future co-workers might proceed. I didn't care what they thought of me. What was wrong with me?

My eyes drifted up to the fifth floor of the eighteenth century building. I stared at the windows and tried to imagine myself behind one of them. I couldn't. Instead, I felt my stomach constrict. Why? Was I suddenly becoming nervous about the meeting? No, that wasn't it. Deep inside me, my heart was yelling, "You'll never work there." But, at the time, my mind discerned it as no more than a faint echo. Its tenor didn't matter. It had been heard.

"Eric?" a voice sounded from the sidewalk.

It was Daniel, a friend of mine from the University. We'd been out of touch for the last two years. "Hey!" I yelled, thrilled to see a familiar face.

He sat down and we caught up on each other's lives. I was so engrossed that I forgot to watch the time. "Oh, shit!" I said, finally looking at my watch. "I'm twenty minutes late for my meeting. Do you want to have lunch later?"

"I'd love to," Daniel said, "but I've got to get going." We exchanged addresses and phone numbers and went our separate ways.

The attorneys and staff in the firm were very cordial and went out of their way to welcome me. I tried to concentrate, to remember names, to read the people I was meeting, but I could not. I would have been more successful trying to listen to, and understand, a speech delivered in Chinese. I knew that this was not for me. What troubled me, however, was why this was happening now. I had made the leap, committing myself to leave Pascal, his brother and the safety of the old firm. The new firm, I now realized, wasn't a forward step; it wasn't even a lateral step. Anything in the legal profession would be a step down from working with Pascal and his brother.

I said my good-byes and raised a few eyebrows when I turned down an offer for lunch. I had to get back to Lyon, I explained. In truth, I wasn't ready to leave Marseilles. In fact, I wasn't ready to take another step. What was the point? I had no idea where I was going. I had thought that I'd laid out the perfect plan. But my angel was telling me loudly and clearly, "Stop thinking and start feeling." And the feeling in Marseilles screamed, "No!"

I drove around the city in search of ... I didn't know what I was looking for—answers, I suppose. But every turn, every intersection led nowhere. I felt nothing in this city but emptiness. It held nothing for me. How could that be? Where else was I supposed to go? I knew it was time to leave Lyon, but if not for Marseilles and the offer by the firm, where and for what? After all, it had been so easy landing the job that I was sure it was a sign from God.

I'd had enough. I followed the signs for the A7, shot onto the autoroute and headed north. Where the hell was I supposed to go? I knew my immediate destination was Lyon, but what was I going to do when I arrived?

Before I knew it, I was pulling off the autoroute, driving through the center of Lyon, and into a space near my office. I sat in the car for several seconds, wondering where the last two hours had gone, wondering if I had really been in Marseilles that morning. What was happening?

Fortunately, there was a great deal of work awaiting me—three files needed immediate attention.

When I got home that night, I told Camille that the meeting went well, but couldn't tell her I was having second thoughts about Marseilles. We had dinner with the children, spoke little and did the dishes together. Camille asked me several times what was wrong and I answered each time that I didn't know. She knew me better than I knew myself and allowed me to work through it.

It was past midnight and I couldn't sleep. My heart was in my throat. Why wasn't the firm in Marseilles good enough? The answer was obvious—Pascal DeLorier was one in a billion. If I was leaving him, I was leaving the law. Then, why wasn't Lyon good enough? There were myriad answers. The only one that mattered was that my gut knew it was time to go. Okay, but where?

I crawled out of bed, threw on a pair of shorts and tee-shirt and headed for my car. I had to get out of Lyon. The answer was out there somewhere.

I raced along the Rhone, returning to the same autoroute I had driven earlier that day. There was no traffic, and, before I realized it, I'd reached two hundred kilometers per hour. I had driven the stretch of autoroute that leaves Lyon hundreds of times. So, why on that night I forgot about the hairpin turn remains a mystery to me.

I was flying down the left lane, coming over a rise, when the enormous yellow arrows pointing left came into view. There was a ninety degree turn to the left two hundred meters away. The problem was, at two hundred kilometers per hour, I was traveling at fifty-five meters per second.

I was strangely serene in that moment. "*Merde*," I said quietly.

In the four seconds I had, I managed to shift from fifth to third. I couldn't slam on the brakes at that speed or I would have lost control.

The engine wailing, almost at the red line, I yanked the wheel to the left. I began the turn, but the car was still going far too fast. I drifted one lane to the right, then a second. I was one lane away from crashing into the cement wall. Keeping control of the car was no longer my number one priority. I didn't want to end up as graffiti on the A7.

Slamming on the brakes, I turned hard to the left. Immediately, the car ceased responding to me and flew into a spin. I wasn't spinning towards the cement wall; instead, I was heading towards the cement median, separating northbound and southbound traffic. After two complete revolutions, the front right bumper slammed into the divider and bounced me back into the middle lanes.

The car finally stopped. Still in third gear, it stalled. I took a deep breath. I was in partial shock. I didn't have time to gather myself, however. I was stopped; worse, I was facing the wrong direction. Bright lights shone on the cement wall. Another vehicle was about to make the turn and, since I couldn't see him, I knew he couldn't see me, either.

I started the engine, shifted into first, and made the most efficient three-point turn of my life. I escaped at the first exit and pulled under a street light. Amazingly, the only damage to the car was a deep scuff of the bumper and spoiler on the front right side. Just then, my knees gave out and I fell to the ground. I began shaking uncontrollably. My adrenaline had been exhausted in a matter of minutes and I was powerless to move.

Sitting on the asphalt, my back against the license plate, I looked up to the sky. I couldn't go any faster. I couldn't go any farther. Every plan, every strategy—everything had failed. "What is it you want?" I yelled. "What do you want from me? You want me to give up? Okay, I give up. You win. Do you hear me? You win. Now, tell me what you want me to do!"

I had always believed in God's will, that God had a plan for us and knew what was best. But that never prevented me from employing *my* plan and simply hoping it was God's as well. I never accepted that we could know what God's will was. We're just supposed to go about our business, hoping that God is on the same page. Besides, the idea of God's will seemed a lot grander than the minutiae of where I lived and what I did to earn a living. Now, however, it was clear to me that God was getting directly involved and blocking my choices about these minutiae. Since the awakening of my spirit and the engagement of my soul, God—through my angel—was talking to me. And as long as my soul knew Marseilles and Lyon were not part of God's plan, I couldn't do it.

"So, what is it?" I asked the sky. "What is your plan? Don't make me guess anymore. I'm tired of running into walls. Just tell me what you want me to do."

The street light went out.

My stomach shrunk. I was frightened. This was the first time I'd gotten angry at God. Maybe, it wasn't the best tack to take. Just as quickly, however, the fear subsided and a peace came over me. I knew that what I was doing was right. In giving up my will to God, I felt empowered. It seems like a contradiction in terms, I know, but that's how I felt. And it seems like the easy thing to do—to give up, to put everything in God's hands. In reality, however, it's the most difficult thing to do. To abandon your fears and thoughts for the unknown is to jump into the void. To allow God to give you what is best is surprisingly terrifying. It is the ultimate leap of faith.

Sitting on the ground, underneath the extinguished street light, against the vehicle in which I had almost died moments earlier, I knew it was right. I felt it in my gut.

"I trust you, God. Help my distrust," I said for maybe the thousandth time in my life, but with a new meaning.

❀　　　❀　　　❀

I sneaked back into bed that night without disturbing Camille. The next morning, just before I went to work, I admitted, "I'm having second thoughts about Marseilles."

Her eyes bulged and her jaw clenched. "We are *not* staying here."

"Did I say that?"

"You're getting cold feet. I knew you'd do this."

"Would you get off my back!" I yelled. "All I said is that I'm not sure about Marseilles. We're going, but I don't know—Never mind." And I left for work.

As occurred nine months earlier, I began going to church several times a day to pray for guidance. The peace of the night before was gone and my insides were in turmoil again. Hadn't I progressed from that first foray nine months ago? Hadn't my decision to give in to God's will been enough? What the hell was going on? I recalled the pain involved in awakening my soul; it seemed to be happening all over again. But, why?

Elisabeth and Christophe returned from their honeymoon. They, along with my sister, Christine, who was between apartments, spent a week with us. They were energized, relaxed and rested—a stark contrast to the ogres that met them at the airport. But their excitement was contagious.

As had happened so many times before, Camille and I were able to empty our hearts onto the table, free of posturing and without bias, since it was not a battle between the two of us. With the third parties present, the level of honesty rose dramatically.

"I can't explain it," I was saying. "When I was in Marseilles, I just knew in my gut that working at that firm was not God's plan. Besides, I'd be nuts to leave Pascal and work for any other attorney."

"But I don't want to stay here," Camille repeated.

"I don't think Eric is saying that you have to stay," Christine intervened.

"We're going," I said. "We are going; we are going; we are going. Okay? God, how many times to I have to say it?"

Camille jumped from her chair, gave me a dirty look, and pounded inside. There was no need to explain to the others left on the balcony where I was going. I found Camille in the kitchen, took her hand and led her to the living room.

"We have to talk," I said. "No bullshit. We have to decide where we're going."

"We *are* going, right?"

"Yes."

"Where?"

"That's the issue."

"Where do you want to go?" asked Camille.

"Where do *you* want to go?"

It was a special moment. We saw it in each other's eyes. There were no games, no facades—we were opening our hearts. We looked at each other. Camille's eyes sparkled. "Why don't we go for the big jump?" she said. "Straight for our dream."

"The Caribbean?"

"Why not?"

I held up my hands. "Yeah, why not? Let's not go halfway this time. It didn't work before."

"Where in the Caribbean?"

"St. Barthélémy," I suggested. I said the two words as though they had been chewed on, contemplated, analyzed and proven true for weeks. It struck me that they had. But, as soon as the words escaped my lips, I realized they hadn't. Where did that come from? I wondered. Instantly, I knew. This was not like Australia or Ré Island. I had asked God where and God answered.

Camille smiled and kissed me. "That's the place I've been thinking about."

We returned outside to tell the others.

Before I could say anything, Camille announced, "I knew we weren't going to Marseilles."

I leaned forward. "Excuse me?"

"I've known for six weeks."

"How?"

"My little voice."

"Damn it, Camille! That isn't fair. You should have told me. How could you keep something like that to yourself?"

Camille burst into tears. "Because I wanted to. I didn't want to give you a reason to stay here."

"Why was it Lyon or Marseilles?" I asked. "I never said that if Marseilles didn't work out, we were going to stay in Lyon."

It was her turn to look at me askance. "The only reason you agreed to go to Marseilles is because you were offered a good job there. It's the job that dictates the location for you, not vice versa."

She was right—at least, partly. What she didn't understand is that my trip to Marseilles and my crash on the autoroute had changed me. I had heard my heart, my soul—I don't know what. But I knew the source. It was supernatural. It said "No" to Marseilles. But that didn't mean "Yes" to Lyon and the same old routine. I was beginning to understand what was happening, as usual, with the benefit of hindsight.

"You're right. If I hadn't gotten the job in Marseilles, we would be staying here until I got a job elsewhere. But that's why it happened the way it did. I had to be brought along slowly. I got the job, was ready to move, and now, not willing to work in the law for anyone other than Pascal, I'll go anywhere. I'll do anything. Which is not something I could have said last March."

"Any idea where?" asked Christophe.

"St. Barthélémy."

"In the Caribbean?" said Elisabeth.

I nodded. "It's where we're supposed to go. I don't know why. I don't know what I'll do there. But, deep inside, I know that's the place." I caught Camille and

Christine staring at each other, Christine's mouth agape. "What?"

My sister turned to me with a big smile. "Camille told me yesterday that she'd like to go to St. Barthélémy. Did you guys talk about it?"

"Inside just now was the first I've heard him mention it," answered Camille. She turned to me, a plea in her eye. "You're serious this time? You're sure?"

"Absolutely."

"You won't change your mind tomorrow?"

"No," I said laughing. "Nothing I've ever decided has felt so right. Except marrying you."

"Have you ever been there?" asked Christophe.

Camille shook her head. "Never. Neither of us."

"Then, that must be the place," he said with a smile.

We toasted the decision and reveled in the craziness of the night. Four children to feed, bills to pay, shelter to obtain—it didn't matter. We were listening to our hearts and to the will of God that echoed therein. It was fun while it lasted.

❀   ❀   ❀

The next morning, Camille and I were not alone in bed. Each of the children had remained in his or her own bed. Instead, it was my doubter that shared my pillow. This time, however, I recognized him. I swore to myself that I would not listen. I was going to follow my heart, regardless of his assault on my mind.

It began in the shower and continued throughout the morning. Every imaginable detail of a transatlantic move ricocheted around my head. The environment of my office did not lend itself to spiritual adventures. My office was the quintessence of the Real World. And it was in the Real World that doubts and fears ruled.

Nobody can just up and leave—especially with four children. That's true, I realized. I hadn't known anyone else who had done it.

You have to have a job before leaving. I couldn't argue with that.

At least, do the math. I grabbed a paper, pen and calculator. I took our equity in the condo, our savings, and subtracted the cost of the move, outstanding bills, three months' expenses on the island. Impossible! Financially, it could not be done.

I wanted to focus on the ultimate goal—the final destination. But the details of how we would get there and what we would do and every other temporal concern haunted me. I found an entirely new meaning in the aphorism: *The devil is in the details.*

I needed help. I called my mother to tell her of the news. She was lukewarm. I called another sister. She was having problems with her boyfriend. I felt a pain overwhelming my heart. I was slipping and I knew it.

Turn it off! I begged my guardian angel. *I know this is right, so, please help me turn off my mind.*

My guardian angel did not turn off my mind. He did something better. He planted a thought in my mind with the power of an atom bomb. *This is your last chance.* I had been logical, calculating, and mindful all my life. Those were adjectives I had always aspired to. Now, I knew it had been to the detriment of my heart, my soul and my relationships with God and everyone around me. I recognized—in my mind—that if I were unfaithful to my heart after such extraordinarily clear messages about Marseilles and St. Barthélémy had been sent, the damage would be irreparable. That thought did not win the battle, but it slowed the blitzkrieg of doubts.

My car was in the shop as a result of my tête-à-tête with the median, so I found myself walking home after a métro ride. I stopped in Place Belle Cour. I stood and looked at the hundreds of passersby, the cars moving in line around the square like a giant centipede. In this city of my birth, I recognized nobody. The surrounding sea of humanity was completely foreign to me. And, yet, these thoughts—these doubts that were plaguing me. They weren't mine. I didn't create them. These strangers did. Why was I listening to beliefs espoused by those people— by society? Shouldn't I create my own beliefs? I had a soul, a mind, and an angel. Why on earth would I choose to abandon them for what everyone else believed?

I walked in the front door feeling stronger. I was winning the battle. In any case, it was Friday night. That was reason enough to be happy.

After dinner, Camille, Christophe, Christine, Elisabeth and I were enjoying a *digestif* on the balcony. We spoke of spirituality and of how far everyone had come in the last year. The portable phone rang and I picked it up.

It was our real estate broker. She had an offer on our condo. Ninety minutes later, we had a contract. There was contingency—the buyers had to sell their home by September 24; but, it was still a contract. If all went well, we would be moving October 28. Camille was thrilled, as were my sisters and Christophe. As for me, gratitude reigned inside my heart. There is no such thing as coincidence. It is a word used by individuals too afraid to see the confluence of the temporal and supernatural. The contract's arrival twenty-four hours after our decision to trust God and to go to St. Barths on a wing and a prayer was divine validation. It wasn't a vision or a voice, but was just as clear. After more than three months of trying to sell our condo, it happened the day after we switched our destination from Marseilles to St. Barths! If the contract had come four weeks earlier, we would have already moved to Marseilles. I had received the sign I needed.

The very next day, however, my pillar of strength crumbled. Camille called her parents to announce our change in plans. She was cross-examined for thirty minutes. "That's crazy," her father said. "Craziness never succeeds. You can't. Not with four children. What's Eric going to do—be a waiter or a doorman? You have to leave with a secure job offer, at the very least."

Camille was reeling for an hour. She hadn't expected the negativity, let alone the effect it had on her. We talked and she seemed to be doing better. Elisabeth, Christophe and Christine were running errands, so it was just Camille and I on the balcony later that afternoon.

"What are you going to do about getting a job?" she asked.

Holding up my hands, I said, "Stop. No details. I'm winning the war in my head. If I get into the details, I'll be finished."

"So, you're just going to go there and hope for the best? What are we going to live on—*d'amour et d'eau fraîche*?"

"If we have to live on love and water, we will. Look, if this is really God's plan for us, the opportunities will be provided."

She shook her head in dismay. "What? You think someone is just going to knock on the door and offer you a job?"

"No, I'll look for a job. But not right now. I can't get into the details. Not yet, anyway."

"You've got to get a job."

"I will."

She set her hands on her hips and tilted her head. She looked like the quintessential disapproving mother. "How?" she demanded.

"I don't know. I can't think about it right now." I rubbed my face. "I can't think at all."

"When are you going to think about it?"

"Come on, Camille, give me a break." I started to walk away.

"Someone has to think about this."

"Fine. *You* think about it."

She blocked my path. "I'm taking care of the children. You have to get a job."

"Today?"

"Soon."

"Don't you want to go? Would you rather stay here?"

"Oh," she said with a sarcastic smile, "we're going. Believe me, we're going. But I'm not going to starve there."

"Don't you trust me?"

"Not when you're so cavalier about earning a living."

"Trust God, at least."

Her sarcastic smile disappeared. She became dangerously serious. "You're not God."

Furious, I stomped inside. Why was she doing this to me? Why was she unraveling several days of hard work? It didn't make sense. We wanted the same thing. She knew that I couldn't get too wrapped up in the details and doubts if I was to follow through with our decision to go. Then, I understood. The reason was right in front of me. For years, she had been pushing me up my mountain of doubts, fears and limiting beliefs. A few days earlier, we reached the summit and I was now rolling down the other side. All the while, busy pushing me, Camille had never faced her own fears. Her father had opened Pandora's box. And out flew a swarm of killer bees.

"Listen," I said, returning to the patio, "don't put your fears or doubts on me."

"What do you mean?"

"I'm not afraid of not getting a job or not making a living. You are. They're *your* fears and doubts. In fact, I don't believe they're yours—they're your fathers. But, if you want to take them on, that's your decision. Just don't impose them on me."

"That's nonsense. I'm worried about the children's welfare and—"

"Cut it out. You weren't worried about any of this until you talked to your father."

"So?"

"So, it's his crap. Don't take it from him. Let him keep it. You don't need those fears and doubts. I know I certainly don't. They haven't done me much good up to now."

Camille protested some more, but not very ardently. She knew. And, typical of my wife, she didn't procrastinate. She attacked. Meditation. Prayer. She also sent back to her father the limiting beliefs, fears and negativity that he tried to send her.

Within twenty-four hours, she was again on board. We were leaving Lyon as well as the caution, the fears and limiting beliefs of others behind. By Sunday afternoon, she had made a list of everything we were going to sell or give away. She'd made a list of movers. She'd even decided to sell her engagement ring.

"Wait a minute," I said. "We're not selling your ring." I picked up her hand and admired it. It was a more than three-carat pear shaped diamond with triangular baguettes. I had gone with my father to pick it out shortly before he died and he had helped me pay for it.

"Why not?"

"Because it's your engagement ring."

"Exactly," she said. "We're married now. I don't need it anymore."

"You can't be serious."

"Eric, what's the point of having this beautiful ring on my finger when we could sell it and invest in a house or even live off the money for a few months?"

I shook my head and turned away. Impossible. I would never sell that ring.

"I know it has a lot of sentimental value for us, but it's just a diamond. It's not our love. It's not a child."

"You've got to give me time to think about it."

"I thought you'd given up thinking," she said with a smirk.

"You don't just stop thinking," I said. "We have a mind and an intellect. They serve a purpose. For years, I analyzed without living. But what you're asking me to do is live without thinking. That's wrong."

"No, I'm not. I've given you very good reasons to sell the ring. Give me one reason why we shouldn't."

"Let me digest it."

"Take all the time you want. I've already decided."

"Don't sell it."

"I love the ring. It's magnificent. And I know what it means to you, having picked it out with your father and all. But it's the right thing to do. If we're really going to get rid of society's limiting beliefs and do our own thing, we've got to do it all the way. Remember what Jesus

said, 'Leave everything and follow me.'" Cédric was crying and Camille left to get him out of bed.

She was wrong. It wasn't the sentimental value of
the ring that bothered me. I was thinking about what
other people would say and what other people wouldn't
say. What kind of a husband—what kind of a man would
they think I was should I be forced to sell my wife's engagement ring? What would my own family say about
it? Additionally, I'd miss the stares Camille attracted
because of the ring. The double-takes, the wide eyes. We
were special; we stood out in a crowd because of that
ring.

I knew these beliefs were pathetic. But I also recognized that I was plugged into them. My negative reaction to my wife's decision to sell the ring was based solely
on these beliefs. I wanted to unplug myself, but how?

"I don't care what other people say or think about
me," I said aloud, looking out the window. "Their opin-
ions don't matter. Power doesn't come from them. Power
comes from inside me. It comes from God's grace and
from doing God's will. Power comes from being true to
myself. And, being true to myself is to be true to God."

So, I've said it. How do I know if I'm unplugged or not?
There was only one way to find out. I picked up the
phone and called my mother. "Guess what? Camille has

decided to sell her engagement ring. I'm taking it to the jeweler's this week to have it appraised."

"You're kidding," she said. "Why is she selling it?"

"Because there's no point in moving to St. Barthélémy with more money on her finger than in our pockets."

"What a woman!"

"Excuse me?" It was not the response I'd expected.

"She's amazing. I don't know many women who'd make that sacrifice or who are that unattached to material possessions. She's incredible."

A negative reaction from my mother was to be my litmus test. In the end, however, I had to be content with just facing my fears and limiting beliefs. It seemed to me that, in just a few minutes, I'd managed to unplug from those limiting, pervasive beliefs.

Not surprisingly, I was feeling very good about myself. And, even less surprisingly, my angel quickly changed that.

On Wednesday, I left for work with a ring in my pocket worth more than my car. I had avoided taking the ring the first two days of the week. I didn't know why, nor did I dwell on it. I was sure, however, that I had unplugged from the notions that power comes from sex and money.

I arrived on time for my appointment at the same *bijoutier* where I'd bought the ring almost nine years earlier. The owner of the boutique, Monsieur Doraye, had died just two months before, so on this occasion, I met with his partner.

Monsieur Doraye had been more than just our family's jeweler; he'd been a close friend. He was one of the forty people I had invited to my wedding. He had cried at my father's funeral, and not just because he lost one of his best customers. He had always told my father and me that he would repurchase any piece we bought for the same price he paid. That was his guaranty of satisfaction and exemplified his reputation as the top jeweler in Lyon.

Monsieur Doraye's former partner and I chatted for fifteen minutes about Monsieur Doraye and I learned for the first time that he'd fought for the Resistance during World War II. He had been a fitness fanatic, vegetarian, and a man of inordinate calm, making his death from cancer all the more difficult to understand.

I wanted to keep talking about anything but the ring. I didn't know what had come over me, but I was petrified. The intercom in his office sounded.

"I have to say hello to some friends. What was it that you needed?"

"That's alright. Go ahead. I'll wait."

"You're sure?"

"Absolutely." I sat there like a child, waiting for the principal to return and announce my punishment. My mouth was arid. I reached hesitantly for the candy dish. I was unsure whether I could take one without asking permission. I risked it, primarily because I needed to lubricate my tongue.

"Now," he said upon his return, "what can I do for you?"

I placed my wife's ring on the blotter between us. He smiled. "What a beautiful piece."

"She'd like to sell it back to you."

His smile disappeared and his manner had a suddenly irritated edge to it. *Damn it!* I thought. I knew he wouldn't be happy about this.

"Doesn't she like it anymore?"

"Oh, she loves it, but we're moving to Marseilles," I lied, "and she doesn't feel comfortable wearing it down there because of all the crime."

"Well, we could make a beautiful necklace from the stones."

"No," I said, "she just wants to sell it."

He examined the stone through his eyepiece. He turned it around and examined it further. Finally, setting it down, he said, "Well, I can't sell it as a ring. What I can do is this—I'll appraise the stones, hold it here on consignment, and then, when we sell the stones as part of another piece, I'll send you a check."

I wanted to protest. What happened to Monsieur Doraye's policy of repurchasing the jewelry? Instead, I thanked him, shook his hand and made for the exit as quickly as possible.

"How much?" Camille asked over the phone.

I stood in my office, gazing out the window. I explained what had transpired.

"But that's not what Monsieur Doraye said."

"I know, but Monsieur Doraye is dead and this other guy is in charge."

"Did you remind him of what Monsieur Doraye promised?"

"No."

"What's the number?"

"Why?"

"I'm going to make an appointment to meet him tomorrow. We need the money before we leave for St. Barths."

"Actually, I don't know if that's a good idea."

"Why not?"

"Because I didn't tell him we were going to St. Barths. I said we were going to Marseilles."

"Ah, Eric! Did you tell him we need the money?"

"No. I said it was because of the crime in Marseilles."

"Shit!" What she was really thinking, however, was: "What a wimp!"

❀   ❀   ❀

The next morning, my duty was clear. I had to call the jeweler and take a stand. Camille was giving up her ring because she believed that we were called to St. Barths by something greater than a mere desire to change locale and climate. She believed it was God's will. She also believed that God helped those who helped themselves. She was attached to the ring for reasons of sentimentality, but not for its material worth or for other peoples' perceptions of her. I, on the other hand, was the opposite.

For me, perceptions were important. Consequently, I was a wreck as I pondered the call.

I waited until 11:30. Finally, I could take the acid in my stomach and my headache no more.

"I'm troubled by our meeting yesterday," I began. "It was always my understanding—see, Monsieur Doraye told my father and me that your firm would always buy back any pieces we purchased from you."

"What do you mean by 'buy back?'" he asked.

"A full refund."

"Well, I can't do that."

"So, Monsieur Doraye's promise won't be honored?"

"He has not been involved in the ownership of the firm for ten years. And, in my inventory now, I have several stones like yours. I have to sell those first."

"That's not what I was led to believe to be the policy."

"Well, I'm trying to help you. I could sell it to a wholesaler, but you'll get nothing near market value. I've offered to appraise it and hold it on consignment. I'm doing you a favor."

That was that. Nothing to do. My wife was livid. I, on the other hand, was obsessed, but not with the ring. I was getting that feeling again. There was something gnawing at my insides. I had to face something new. I was growing tired of this cycle—uneasiness; then prayer and meditation; then breakthrough; then solution; then peace; then, uneasiness; then prayer ... When was it going to end? Why did everything have to come piecemeal?

I didn't have to spend much time deciphering the problem. It was this damn childlike mentality I still had. Growing up, I had always been reminded that a child had to respect and be deferential to adults. Politeness made sense. But I had to be respectful of adults who deserved no respect, not from a child nor an adult. I had carried this belief with me into adulthood. I still had unnatural respect for those adults whom I knew when I was a child. I still saw myself as a child vis-à-vis certain people. The best example was Pascal. I had known him since I was five or six. And, now that I was working for him (although he preferred that I say "*with* him"), I still called him Monsieur DeLorier. I not only sought out his counsel, but I yearned for his criticism. It was not that I was a masochist. I just wanted my perception of the relationship reinforced. He was the person in whose presence I most felt like a child. After all, he had replaced my father as head of the firm and as my boss. But more than that, he was one of the few people I knew who really deserved respect. He was simply a good person through and through. He refused to feed my self-imposed status of child. In my eight years working for him, he never once criticized me. Despite being in a position to take advantage of my limiting perception, he forced me to see myself as an adult—to see myself as he saw me. In anyone else's hands, I would have been abused and the perception reinforced.

The confrontation with the jeweler brought this to the surface. I had diagnosed the problem. But, what was the remedy? I talked to Camille and Elisabeth. Both understood; neither had a remedy.

A day after I called the jeweler to make my belated stand, I went to church in the late afternoon. The perception I'd been carrying was like a recently discovered tumor. I wanted to get rid of it. I knew that I had to obliterate it before leaving for St. Barths. Thanks to Pascal's goodness, I had discovered the problem without anyone taking advantage of it. I couldn't work for someone else until I was free of the perception.

I knelt down in a pew and glared at the monstrance on the altar holding the blessed sacrament. The blood was flowing to my head.

"Enough!" I yelled in prayer. "No more games. No more little steps. Show me! I want the whole truth, not bits and pieces of it. Pull down the veil—the *entire* veil."

You wouldn't be able to handle it, I heard in my head.

"I don't care if the truth knocks me on my ass. I don't care if I'm in a coma for two months. I've had enough of these damn games. I've had enough of this cycle and the aggravation and the slow, painstaking process. I want it all. Once and for all!"

I continued emptying my frustration and anger on God for another fifteen minutes. I left, not feeling relieved, but not feeling guilty either. I expected some guilt. This was, after all, just the second time I'd ever gotten angry at God. I wondered if my answer would come as quickly as it did the last time I got angry—after my spin-out on the *autoroute*.

No answer was granted me. I continued chewing on this problem of my child/adult perception. It continued upsetting my stomach. In retrospect, the reason I did not receive an immediate answer was because the ongoing issue prompted me to meditate like never before. I began meditating on a nightly basis—sometimes twice a day. I wanted an answer. I wanted the truth. I wanted to know how to rid myself of this perception. *God, my angel, please show me how to unplug my energy from this limiting belief and plug into the belief that I have nobody above me except God.* I said those words at the beginning of my meditation for the first week. Then, in the second week, I added the following: *Or, just unplug it for me. Do to me what-*

ever is necessary. The meditations during those two weeks provided invaluable insights. I had already given up my will for God's, but it wasn't until I meditated about what that meant that a true acceptance found its way into my heart.

In all my years of dreaming of becoming a full-time writer, I had picked out a path and plan that society had already marked. Write something commercial, I'd been advised. Check out the best-seller's list and pick a similar genre or story. Then, get a literary agent. Then, get a publisher. Then, a book contract. The book won't be published for at least a year, so you'll have to wait to see the sales generated by the book. Then, if the numbers are high enough, you get a second book contract, and, *then*, you can become a full-time author. Where was there room in this plan for a miracle? I'd planned—using society's map—each step towards my destination. I didn't allow for God to intervene anywhere along the way. It was time, I realized, to choose a destination or goal and to leave the "how" up to God. It was time for a leap of faith. The problem was, however, that making a leap of faith, leaving the how up to God, was much easier if the leap occurred at a singular moment in time. It was a lot more difficult in terms of my writing or moving to St. Barths. Each day was a leap of faith. Each day—every minute of it—I had to trust God to provide the how.

That is where meditations, mass and support from Camille, my brothers, sisters and mother were crucial. Everyone I talked to about St. Barths or about becoming a full-time writer seemed to be one of society's soldiers, doing everything he or she could to push me back onto the paved path of society. Even my brother-in-law laughed at my goal of writing—everyone and her uncle wants to be a full-time writer, he'd said. News of our decision to move to St. Barths without any job prospects aroused more than skepticism; it aroused anger. They could not allow for any defections. What would happen if everyone eschewed the paved path? Why isn't the paved path good enough for you? What makes you so special? Insanity was often an answer. Others, unaware of our financial situation, assumed that we were wealthy enough for me to retire at age thirty-one. There simply could not be another reason for making such decisions. "You've lost your mind," one person said. I thought about it for a few seconds, smiled, and responded, "Yes, you're right. I've finally lost my mind."

Part of my therapy, I decided, was to face the fears. I tried to unplug from the fears. I affirmed aloud to myself every day that I wasn't a child, that I trusted God, that I need not fear anyone else. But, it wasn't working. So, I decided to beat my fears into submission. And, after the embarrassing debacle with the jeweler, I was going to be true to myself—true to the truth. I was never again going to lie about what I was planning for fear of somebody's reaction—even an adult's!

The first step was calling the head of the firm in Marseilles. I was nervous. I worried about his reaction. My fears were exacerbated by my inability to reach him for three days. When I did manage to call while he was in the office, I told him that I was not going to accept his job offer, that I appreciated his kindness, and that I was moving to St. Barths with no job and no idea what I'd be doing there. I explained that I realized the last time I was in Marseilles that if I were going to leave Pascal's firm, I was also going to leave the practice of law. He was surprised, but not overly so. He admitted that my decision was going to make him rethink his plans. He was sixty-four, had been thinking about retiring, but planned on sticking around to bring me into the fold. That was no longer necessary.

The next step was to tell Pascal. His father had just died. He and his brother had been absent from the office. When they returned, I announced my change in plans. Pascal was understandably shocked, full of questions, and full of support. He mentioned that he, too, had had thoughts when he was my age of doing something other than the law. He didn't have a desire or passion for any other field, however. I realized at that moment why Pascal was so unflappable, wise and kind. He, unlike so many others in our profession, had asked himself the questions. He hadn't followed society's path blindly. He knew what he wanted, and, with faith, pursued it. He told me that he was sure everything would work out wonderfully for us in St. Barths. A week later, Pascal told me that he received a call from the attorney in Marseilles, questioning whether I was just trying to appease him by saying I was going to St. Barths and really going to work for another firm. Pascal laughed, recounting the story. "He just can't believe it." Once again, off-road trekking was an inconceivable alternative to society's freeway.

With each person whom I told about our change of plans, my fears subsided. I was beating them into oblivion through constant confrontation. What others thought no longer mattered to me. Nevertheless, the daily battles against society's legions waged on. There were skirmishes won and skirmishes lost. But putting myself in God's hands during my meditations at the end of each day healed my wounds and made me stronger. I had a profound sense of gratitude each night that I laid my head down on the pillow. I was at peace and feeling good about myself. In case you haven't picked up on the pattern, it was time for my angel to initiate another earthquake.

❀   ❀   ❀

I had begun penning this manuscript shortly after Camille and I decided to go to St. Barths. I wanted to put down on paper what had happened in the previous nine months, and, sensing the intensity that our actual move to St. Barths would entail, I wanted to preserve my lessons and experiences based on my current perspective, without being tainted by time and the experiences that awaited us on the other side of the Atlantic.

Camille was the only person I allowed to review these pages as they were produced. As always, her support, encouragement and understanding of my commitment to my mistress—my computer—were vital. Every weekend, I printed out my latest additions and turned them over for her perusal. On Saturday night of the last weekend of the summer, Camille settled into bed next to me with the last fifteen pages and began devouring them. The last scene concerned my visit to the jeweler. She rolled over to face me.

"You didn't tell me about this."

"What are you talking about? Of course, I did."

"Not that you were that much of a wimp."

"I explained that I felt like a kid. I may not have gone into as much detail as I did when I wrote it, but you got the gist of it."

She looked at me with a mix of pity and disgust. "Wow."

"What?"

"I can't believe you."

"What do you want me to say? I felt like a child. I'm dealing with it."

"It's more than that."

I waited, hating when she did this—throwing out a statement that begged for further explanation, but not offering any. "Go ahead. Tell me."

"It was about money."

"It had nothing to do with money," I said.

"It had everything to do with money."

"Whatever." I turned my back and fell immediately asleep.

It was a night straight out of hell. Saturday had been summer's last hurrah, with temperatures over thirty-three degrees Celsius and heavy humidity. We did not have air conditioning, so we removed the covers from our bed and left the windows open. In the early morning hours of Sunday, fall arrived with trumpets blaring. The temperature dropped nineteen degrees, lightning struck all around us, and thunder reverberated throughout the house. By three in the morning, two of our children had joined us, while Cédric and Pierre somehow slept through the noise. The storm, chilly air, and children sleeping atop me were inconsequential compared to my dreams. Camille's comment about money sparked a litany of dreams that tortured me all night.

I awakened at six, got up, made a feeble attempt at getting dressed, for no reason other than to stop the dreams. I couldn't force my body to function. Reluctantly, I returned to bed.

When I awakened two hours later, I was a zombie. The message of my dreams hit me with a power and clarity that made the thunder and lightning of the storm seem like a fog horn and pilot light of a distant tug boat dimmed by a dense fog.

Camille took one look at me and asked, "What's wrong?"

I shook my head in dismay. "You were right. It is about money. I dreamed about it all night long. Money, to me, is power."

People respected money. And, even if we didn't have much, people thought we did because of Camille's ring. That's what counted—perceptions. Power was yours if people perceived you as wealthy or sexy. Those are the sources of power, after all—money and sex. I knew it from my own experience. My boss had power over me, even if he didn't use it. He had money and he determined how much I made. Publishers and literary agents also had power over my dream—they decided whether or not I became a full-time writer. Anyone with more money than I, or with the ability to decide how much money I earned, had power over me. Why has the man always occupied a higher position in society and the family?—because he earns the money. Such is the nature of our world. And, then, there is sex. A husband's power is offset only by his wife's power from sex. If she decides when, where and how to have sex, she has the power; that is, unless infidelity is an option. In that case, the mistress has the power. It's perhaps too general, but nonetheless generally true.

Looking at society, it was clear to me. Typically, money is man's weapon and sex is woman's. Regardless of the gender, however, the wealthier, the sexier—the more powerful.

"If I don't have money, then I don't have power, then, I'm just a child," I explained to Camille. "At the same time, I feel like a child; therefore, I don't deserve power; therefore, I'm not entitled to have any money." It was suddenly patently obvious. I understood why I couldn't unplug my energy from the misconception that I was a child among adults. That was only the first half of the equation. The other half was my perception that money is power. The biggest problem was that I didn't want that kind of power. More importantly, God and my angel were not going to allow me to attract money as long as money meant power to me. Any relief arising out of this discovery paled next to the danger of maintaining such a perception. I had to change my beliefs. Recognizing how I perceived money and myself, I couldn't waste any time changing the perception.

Not more than fifteen minutes after descending from my bedroom, I returned upstairs for a meditation. The meditation calmed me, and, just as I was ready to stop, a thought came to me. I remembered a book I had purchased six months earlier, but had not yet read. It was about magnetizing and drawing to you what you desire.

I hadn't read the book because I knew the time was not right. Now, evidently, it was.

Before I could dive into the book, we had several chores to perform. We had leased a small storage unit while our condo was for sale, because the real estate broker judged that our condo was too cluttered. Since our condo was under contract, we decided to vacate the unit. Upon discovering all that we had in storage, we realized that next to nothing was worth shipping to St. Barths. Nevertheless, there remained several large boxes which we hauled back to our condo.

After I had carried everything inside, I sat down in the kitchen with the book and a beer. Camille passed by carrying two boxes of beach towels that my mother had sent us.

"Thank you," she said.

"I'm sorry. Do you want a beer, too?"

"Thank you for carrying these upstairs."

My blood boiled as I waited for her to return.

"The hell with you," I said. "The only reason you said that was to make me feel guilty."

"These boxes have been sitting in the foyer for a week. Don't tell me you didn't see them."

"Why couldn't you take them upstairs?"

"Because it's your job."

"Bullshit! You just wanted to make me feel guilty."

An hour later, I was still inside. The last exchange had sapped my desire to read. Instead, I got lost in a soccer game on television. Camille arrived in the living room where I was sitting. "I have to go to the supermarket."

"Okay."

"Do you want to come with me?"

It was a loaded question. She always wanted me to join her. "No."

Her look said it all. As if not enough, she crossed her arms and said, "Are you just going to sit in front of the television all day?"

"Maybe."

With a huff, she stomped off. My saving grace was the fact that Cédric was still napping. Five minutes later, however, we heard him cooing through the monitor.

"Cédric is up," Camille called to me.

"I'll get him."

"Are you sure you don't want to come to the supermarket?"

"I'm sure."

Again, her irritation was evident as she departed. I sat on the balcony with Cédric and Pierre. I read the book, hungry for some clue as to how to change this perception I had. When Camille returned, we unloaded the groceries, then, she joined me outside.

"I need your help," I began. "I can't figure out how to change this damn perception I have. People with money have power. I don't have money, so, I don't have power."

"But you earn more than most people."

I shook my head. "That's the point. I don't want that kind of power—I mean, I don't want power if it comes from money. So, even though I earn a big paycheck, money and I are like two magnets that reject each other."

"But what does that have to do with feeling like a child?"

"A child, according to my perception, is someone without power. It's a vicious circle. On the one hand, I feel like a child, so I don't feel I deserve power, so I don't attract that which gives power—money. On the other hand, I don't want power if it comes from money, so I push away money, and end up feeling like a kid—powerless."

"I don't understand."

"You don't?"

"I understand the words; I don't understand your feelings. I'm just the opposite. I don't want people to think or know that I have money. I don't like the awe that my ring evoked in other people."

"So, you can't help me?"

She shrugged.

"I just realized something. You've known how I feel even before I knew what I felt. And you've capitalized on it. I've felt like a kid, so you've treated me like a kid. You've used this perception to gain power over me."

That crooked smile of hers appeared suddenly. "I know. When I left for the supermarket, I felt terrible about earlier—the comment about taking the boxes upstairs and making you feel guilty about not coming to the supermarket. I'm sorry. I'll try to stop it."

"It's not about you, Camille. It's my problem. It's not your fault I feel like a kid. Although, I will admit you're a sly fox for using it against me." That earned me a smile. "But even if you stopped treating me like a kid, that doesn't mean I'll stop perceiving myself as a kid. And that won't stop me from perceiving money as the source of power."

"So, what can I do?"

"Help me figure out how to change my perception."

"Eric, I don't know. I'd like to help you, but I just don't understand why you feel the way you do."

I was obsessed. As discoveries about me went, this was enormous. It explained so much. My salary had increased more than threefold in the last seven years, but our financial situation got dimmer and dimmer because I was repelling money—first, because that wasn't the kind of power I wanted; second, because I didn't see myself as worthy of any power. My foray into energy work in February, trying to force the agent in Paris to sign me up didn't work because, deep inside, I believed she had a power that I didn't. Moreover, I had limited how my dreams would be realized instead of leaving the "how" up to God. And, I realized, God would never give me a book contract, money or any part of my dreams as long as my old fears and perceptions would distort the meaning and value of the gift. I was sabotaging my present and future by limiting myself to the past. I was living the life of a thirty-one year old husband, father of four and writer based on the beliefs, fears and perceptions of a ten year-old. I knew what had to be done. But how was again the issue.

❀   ❀   ❀

Before things improved, they got much worse. Camille was looking for a fight. I was completely obsessed with fixing my internal wiring. The children were on a rampage—either destroying, screaming, crying, fighting or disobeying. They were reacting to us, but it didn't make their behavior any less aggravating.

"What's wrong with you?" I asked Camille for the tenth time, just as we were about to sit down for dinner.

"I keep looking up at that calendar on the wall. And, as big as a neon sign, I see *September Twenty-Fourth: End of Contingency Period.* That's less than three weeks away, Eric. What happens if they don't sell their house? I don't want to spend another winter in Lyon."

"Would you cut it out? There's nothing we can do about it. It's in God's hands. Worrying about it won't make it sell."

Camille had been growing more and more edgy as the school year approached. Now, she had me worried. I felt my trust slipping away. The details were getting in the way again. The high season in St. Barths began on November 1. If we didn't close on our house on October 28, my job prospects would be even more limited. For the first time since that fear-filled week after deciding to go to St. Barths, I was scared.

That night, after Camille and the children were asleep, I meditated. It was one of the most proactive meditations I had experienced. I employed the magnetizing technique from the book I was reading. I imagined a coil coming out of my heart, circling my body and rising above my head. I asked God to give me grace, divine energy and love. After the white light filled my body, I directed it into the coil. I clarified the essence of what I wanted—the ability to empower others through my words, full days with my wife and children, a white, open house with a pool overlooking the Caribbean, the freedom to travel, the freedom to continue on this spiritual journey, the freedom to write, to write, to write. I felt what it would be like to experience all that. The coil acted as an energy magnet to draw to me that which I sought. Suddenly, it was like I was watching a movie at ten times normal speed. Visions, pictures and sounds came to me, one after another, too quickly for my brain to grasp each one. When the energy in the coil subsided, so did the visions. I went to sleep immediately after the meditation. I probably should have done something to stop the magnetism, because within two hours, three of our four children made their way into our bed.

The next day, this manuscript was on hold. I had arrived at present day and was waiting for the future to unfold, to give me the material about which I would write.

I called Elisabeth in Paris and told her about the magnetism technique I was employing. She had recently quit her job as a teacher and had begun writing full-time. Her response to my news was a mix of disinterest and disdain.

"What's wrong?" I asked.

"You have to get to the point where you don't need to magnetize what you want."

"Why?"

"Because it's unnecessary," she said.

"I don't get it. If you don't magnetize, then how do you obtain what you want?"

"I don't know. You just live it. You manifest it."

"What does that mean?"

"I can't explain it," she said.

"But, it's making me feel the power inside. It's helping me realize that power doesn't come from other people."

"Well, if it's helping you, that's good."

Irritated, I hung up. I didn't mind the criticism, but I would have liked a little more help. If not magnetizing, then what?

That night, my attention turned from myself to Camille. In truth, I was concerned for her as much out of love as out of fear. She had been spinning farther and farther out of control. Her mood was dark and edgy. She had been terribly congested for two weeks and it was getting to the point where she couldn't sleep. For two days, her eyes had been red, irritated and tearing. I knew something was going on inside her. She denied it. If she continued to refuse to investigate, I feared that it would affect our future and limit us in terms of leaving for St. Barths.

We put the children to bed, opened a bottle of wine, and Camille poured out her heart—albeit unintentionally.

"You're hot," I said, admiring her body.

"God, I'm so sick of people telling me how good I look *considering* I've had four children."

"I didn't say that."

"Not you. Everyone else. I'd like to look good—period. But, it's always with a qualification."

"Who cares what other people think?"

"I know," she said, "but it bothers me. Sometimes, when I'm walking around with the children—this is terrible to admit, but I'm embarrassed to be with them. I think people are looking at me as just a baby machine."

That triggered a thought. "You know the other night when I told you how gorgeous you were and you didn't care? You said that I'm the only one who has ever told you that you're beautiful."

"So?"

"We're right back to the same issue. You want recognition from other people."

"I know. But it doesn't mean anything because my status is mother, not just a woman."

I smiled at her. "We've had this discussion before. Only the last time it was about intelligence. You didn't think anybody recognized your intelligence. Nothing has changed. Just the basis for recognition."

"But I work out all the time and my butt is still fat."

I laughed. "Keep saying it and you'll make it come true."

"And every time I call my sister, all I hear from her is how thin she is, how many guys look at her in the street, that so-and-so told her she should go into modeling. I can't stand it."

I leaned forward and set my arms on the table. "Listen to yourself. You're angry at your sister because she craves recognition."

"And?"

"You're angry, because it's a reflection of you. She wants other people's recognition, as do you, and you don't like seeing yourself through her."

"But she's always done that. So have my parents. Growing up, it was always about what this person or that person said about us."

"So, unplug. You don't have to maintain that belief anymore—that other people's recognition is important."

"But I've never gotten recognition."

"Of course not," I said. "You're not going to get recognition, because that's not what you need. What you need is to recognize yourself—to love and value yourself. Other people's recognition is worthless. At some level, you already realize that."

"No, I don't."

"Hell, Camille, you couldn't have picked a more obvious example. Everyone thinks you're one of the most beautiful women in the world—pre- or post- children. So, even though you say you want recognition, you don't. Because you've got it and it doesn't make a whit of difference. What you really want is to recognize yourself."

"I'll tell you what I recognize—I've got a big butt."

"And as long as you keep saying it, it will be true. You're creating reality. You don't recognize your own internal and external beauty. Consequently, you're going to have a body or a soul or whatever, exactly as *you* see it. *You*—not anybody else."

We spoke for another hour, going at her recognition problem from every angle. It was exciting. She wasn't defensive. On the contrary, she was anxious to solve it. I garnered that she was feeling differently about herself later, as sex that night was truly extraordinary.

Despite Elisabeth's disdain for the technique, after Camille was asleep, I meditated, again magnetizing what I wanted. And, again, I went to sleep without fully pulling out of the meditation. By two in the morning, three of our children had again been drawn into our bed. Even thunderstorms brought no more than two children into bed with us.

I awakened exhausted. I had come to learn that my energy in the morning, or lack thereof, was not dictated by the number of hours I slept. It was rather a reflection of my inner workings. I knew something was wrong. I realized that I had been feeling out of sorts for two days— since I began magnetizing. The sense of power I enjoyed from magnetizing was, alone, changing my perceptions about money as a source of power. Not just in my head but in my heart, I was discovering that real power comes from God. And, in my case, the power was my words. So, why were my desires to be a full-time author, more particularly, the desire to be a full-time author in St. Barths, bothering me so much?

I was in my office by six-thirty in the morning. Camille called me and I explained my newest funk. She laughed. "Now you're the one worrying about the details. Trust."

I hung up the phone, took a sip of coffee and stared at a picture of Angélique and Pierre taken a few years back on a beach. Their eyes penetrated to my soul. I began wondering what was different about St. Barths versus Lyon. I wasn't thinking about the physical differences; I was thinking about the differences for me. It was just another place and another job to fill time until the dream of being a full-time writer was realized—was handed to me. I was making a leap of faith, but that leap of faith dealt with getting a job on St. Barths and not starving to death. That wasn't much of a leap of faith when I looked closely. I was bright, able-bodied, and bilingual. We would always get by. So, what was to be different about this move? What was going to be the difference between St. Barths, Marseilles and Lyon? Nothing, I realized. It was just another excuse to stall my dream, my passion, my vocation.

Camille kept coming to mind. At first, I thought it was our intimate encounter that demanded my attention. I was all too happy to entertain the memory. But that wasn't it. It was the conversation that preceded it. The conversation with Camille made everything clear. It was as close to a "Eureka!" moment as I've ever had. All I had to do was take my advice to Camille and apply it to myself. I had been waiting for years for someone to recognize me as a full-time writer. I had been waiting for someone to recognize my writing and publish my books. It was the same malaise that plagued my wife. I was seeking approval, permission, recognition ... from others.

What an ingrate! I thought. God had given me this passion and a talent for writing. How ungrateful I was for ignoring God's gifts and waiting instead for someone else to tell me I was a writer. It was akin to what I realized months earlier about self-love: If God loves you, who are you to say that you don't deserve to be loved? This time, it was: If God has given you a talent or passion, who are you to set it aside, say it's not good enough, and wait for someone else to tell you it is or to give you what you *really* need?

No more, I decided. I had been waiting for some-body else to alter my reality. It was time to make my own reality.

The time is now. The past is of no use to me. The future isn't promised. All I have is today. I decided that I was going to St. Barths as a full-time writer. How? I didn't know. I would leave that up to God. I would remain vigilant and open. As I had learned from Michel, I would look for the extraordinary in the ordinary. But, I was sure of one thing—no matter how, it would happen. It was as simple as that. I was creating my own reality just as easily and simply as I created a story on paper. And, so, in mid-September, for the first time in the writing of this story, I set forth the future instead of recounting the past:

The day of departure—October 28—will arrive. The pre-vious weeks and months will have been the most intense leg of my spiritual journey to date.

There will be no "job" waiting for me in St. Barths, be-cause I won't need one. I will finally be a full-time writer.

Sitting in the airport departure lounge, Camille's eyes will swing between our children motoring around the other passengers and the listing of houses for sale on St. Barths. She will be excitedly planning which houses we'll visit.

I'll smile. It was all so simple. Looking back on the previous year, I'll note how I constantly updated my impression of how much I knew—about God, about our connection to God, and about life itself. At that moment, sitting in the airport, it will seem like I know a great deal. Certainly, I'll know a lot more than I did a year ago. But, I will also recognize that the next twelve months will prove that at that moment, I'm an ignoramus. So be it. I'll be happy where I am. And, I'll be excited about whatever adventure there might be waiting for us out there.

❀   ❀   ❀

An ignoramus? You bet!

After penning what I wanted the future to manifest, I put the manuscript aside. I thought it was done. It was proof that, after learning so much, I'd really learned nothing. Okay, not *nothing*. Let's just say that I was still learning. And, of course, I'll always be learning. But I wasn't *living* the very lessons I could verbalize and about which I had written.

Camille and I were both confident that the future was bright. We both believed that we would be in St.

Barths on October 28 and that I'd finally be a full-time writer, just as I'd written. This faith was a blessing. Rather than concentrating on the future and what it might or might not be, we concentrated more on today.

"Lyon isn't so bad," Camille's little voice had told her countless times over the years. She had been afraid that it meant she had to stay in Lyon. Now that she knew she was definitely leaving, she took it to heart. She enjoyed Lyon like she had never enjoyed it before. We both did.

Every weekend we headed to Annecy or to the park or up to Fourvière. We made the most of every moment. We didn't even notice the days going by. When September twenty-fourth rolled around without word from our buyers, it was almost a shock. I received a call from their lawyer asking for an extension of the contract. What choice did we have? There were no other buyers knocking down our door. October 28 was suddenly an impossibility. That meant that winter would arrive before we left.

Strangely, we were not upset. If our departure was to be delayed, so be it. After all, I'd learned in February not to place arbitrary deadlines on God. Time was a physical measurement of man, not a constraint of the spirit.

In our euphoria about moving to Marseilles or the tropics, we had given most of our winter clothing to the poor. Refusing to put any credence or energy into scarcity ("scare city"), we concluded that those gifts were meant to be, and purchased the bare essentials as the need arose.

October passed with remarkable rapidity. We enjoyed each day, both the people we encountered and the change of seasons. With each passing day, however, came the question, *Why are we still here?* It wasn't asked out of bitterness, but rather out of a genuine curiosity, the underlying assumption of which was that there was a reason for our delay. We simply sought to understand what that reason was. What was the next lesson we had to learn?

I was driving home on October 27. Traffic was terrible as we'd just turned our clocks back and it was already dark at six. My thoughts, however, were far away from the cars creeping around me. What was I supposed to do? What didn't I understand?

God helps those who helps themselves. Ask and you shall receive. The crush of the biblical cliches wasn't helping.

I had tried to help myself. I had asked, but I hadn't received. Actually, that wasn't true. I hadn't received what I'd asked for—to be a full-time writer. But each day brought me some blessing.

"Surrender!" I heard. "Would you just surrender!" Surrender *what?* I wondered.

I was willing to leave the *how* up to God. What else was I supposed to... That was it, wasn't it? I was so proud of myself for leaving the *how* up to God, but I hadn't been ready to give up dictating the *what*. Was I ready now? Could I honestly say, "I'm ready for whatever is best. I know what I want, but I'll accept whatever's best."? Why not? What choice did I honestly have?

"Camille!" I yelled upon opening the front door, not even taking the time to remove my coat, "I'm not sure St. Barths is where we're supposed to go."

Her face instantly tightened. It was not enough that she'd just spent three hours with four screaming maniacs who, due to the cold weather, hadn't been able to unwind outside. Now, her husband was dashing her dreams and her plans. "Don't do this to me," she pleaded.

I took her face in my hands, my euphoric smile tranquilizing her. "How do we know where we're supposed to go? Really. How do we know what's best for us?"

"We have to choose *somewhere*."

"I know," I said, excitedly. "But there's a reason, or reasons, our condo hasn't sold yet. Let's not waste any more time dictating the details. I'm open to anything. I'd like to be a full-time writer, but, if we get to St. Barths or wherever tomorrow, and I'm not, I'll work as a fisherman or a waiter or ... *whatever!* I'll be a full-time writer when the time is right and not a minute before."

"What does that have to do with St. Barths?" she asked, less nervously than I'd expected.

"Our destination is just another detail. Let's be open. Let's ask for guidance. If St. Barths isn't right for us at this time in our lives, we'll either screw up by forcing our way there or we'll waste time by waiting for it to happen."

"So, where?"

"Wherever!" I was excited. It felt right. I knew that this was the way to go. How foolish I'd been. I would do anything for my children. I would die for them; I would circle the world for them; I would fight for them. All, because I love them. Why had I questioned God's love for me? Why had I limited what God would do for me? I shook my head and smiled. Because I didn't deem myself worthy. Because I thought I knew what was best. And, because I didn't trust that God wanted my happiness. Fortunately, my guardian angel had assiduously plagued me until I gave up and finally allowed God to love me and do for me what God knew best.

Camille was noncommittal. She didn't argue, but she didn't jump for joy.

The next evening, October 28, Angélique's birthday, I arrived home to find Camille pale, her eyes bloodshot.

"What's wrong?" I asked. "Rough day?"

"I spent an hour this afternoon talking to God," she said, a brilliant smile on her otherwise drained face.

"And?"

"I give up, too." She started crying, in complete release, not anguish, and threw her arms around me.

"I'm proud of you," I said.

"I love you."

"I love you, too."

Camille returned to the kitchen to finish preparing dinner. I sat down in the living room with a grin goofy enough to compete with Pierre.

"Why are you smiling, daddy?" asked Angélique, climbing onto my lap.

"Because I love you, princess."

She pulled several strands of hair to her mouth. "I love you, too," she said shyly.

"Happy birthday, sweetheart. My big six year-old!"

She reached her arms around my neck and squeezed.

"Thank you, Angélique."

"For what? The hug?"

"No, thanks for choosing me as your father."

Her blue eyes twinkled. "You're welcome, daddy." She turned, dropped off my knees and ran over to her three brothers who were starting to tear open her gifts.

To think this had all started with her birth! I didn't recognize the Eric Pétris in the delivery room on October 28 six years ago. He was dead. The fears, beliefs and limitations that paralyzed his heart and imagination were gone. Like a tree, pruned and stripped naked by winter, a new, fuller person emerged in the spring. And for the first time in my life, I was truly enjoying the current season without thinking or worrying about the next. Why should I worry? It was in God's hands.

Later that night, after the birthday festivities had ended and the children were corralled into bed, I returned downstairs. I couldn't sleep. I was so grateful for everything that had happened and for the wife and children who blessed me. I was totally wired and energized. I had to express in words what I was feeling. So, I pulled out pen and paper.

I can think, I can run, I can hide;
Deep or shallow, far or near, narrow or wide;
It matters not, for when I stop, he is still beside.

I dive into bed, cover myself from head to feet;
But, as slumber arrives, he yanks the sheet;
Once again, this night like last, sleep will not be mine;
For he is there to prevent peace in my position supine.

Ah, but I have a secret weapon—routine is my shield;
I follow the path of the familiar, careful to never drift far
afield;
It is in my fortress of routine that I can finally own tranquility;
I willingly exchange for these high walls my liberty, my
agility.

Yet, despite a moat as vast as the sea;
He breaches the ramparts and again torments me;
This game of hide and seek I just cannot win;
But I am not of the ilk that easily gives in.

So, I fight, I wage war, no thought of the infernal white
flag;
But he outflanks me, he exhausts me—my will begins to
lag;
I contemplate the impossible—that cursed, hateful word;
I loathe myself for it, but in the end, lay down my sword.

"Stop," I scream, "I give up, I quit, I surrender."
But my angel's comportment is not that of a vanquisher;
His white wings embrace me, a tear of joy falls from his
chin;
"Congratulations," he rejoices, "At last, my friend—you
win!"

AFTERWORD

So, what happened? Where did we end up? Did I become a full-time writer? As of the writing of these words, I do not know. You are, however, holding a clue in your hands; and, in your heart, you're holding the answer that it all worked out perfectly—better, in fact, than any human being could have planned.

DayBue Publishing Ink

Our publising house is committed to publishing works of literary art that have the potential to illuminate and awaken the hearts and minds of all readers.

San Francisco Office:

2107 Van Ness Avenue
Suite 104
San Francisco, CA 94109

Tel: (415) 923-9501
Fax: (415) 923-9531

SURRENDER can be ordered
from the following bookstores:

Read All About It--Toll free (888) 708-BOOK

Ex Libris Bookstore--Toll free (800) 576-0633

Chapter One Bookstore--(208) 726-5425 or
website: www.chapteronebookstore.com
e-mail: Chapter One@chapteronebookstore.com